ISLAND OF SECRETS

EXPEDITION INC. >>> BOOK ONE

J BECKETT

CONTENTS

DEDICATION

I couldn't keep telling stories without the support of my amazing wife, Nicole.

INTRODUCTION

Welcome to the Expedition Inc. Family
New Hire Orientation Starts Now

When you're done reading, I hope you'll take a minute to leave
a review!

PART 1

ONE

RECON

"Take it slow. We don't know how many are home," Jason Kincaid, team leader of *Expedition, Inc.*, said as he and his colleague crept out of the ocean, water dripping off of their matte black scuba gear, built in electronics masking them from any sensors that the pirates might have set up along the beach. Jason was fairly sure their targets had not set up that kind of tech, but better safe than sorry.

Over their comms, Scarlet Jones, the team's resident hacker and computer expert, warned, "According to our intel, most of them should be on their ship. That party barge we set up as a decoy was just too juicy."

Jason looked to his companion. "Okay, move."

"Can't wait to do some serious damage to these assholes," Sofia Gomez said, her mirrored face mask hiding her face but doing nothing to hide the glee in her voice.

Jason shook his head. "Down, girl. We're being paid to recon these pirates, nothing more."

"Then why do we have guns?" the ex-marine next to him said, her pace quickening. Their suits had already shed the water that was clinging to them and had a matte dry look that reflected no light.

The island of North Coronado was technically in Mexican territorial waters—technically. After the collapse of the Mexican government, the US and the remnants of that government had been debating for years who should police the area while leaving it alone. The Mexican Navy lacking the manpower, and the US Navy lacking the interest, made the situation a win for pirates. Over the last year, pirates had taken over the uninhabited northernmost island in the small Coronado Island chain off the coast of Mexico, spitting and striking distance from the US—something several civilian pleasure and freight vessels had recently learned, the hard way. Which was why Jason and his team were there, to find the pirates' base so the Navy could swoop in.

The Navy hired Jason and his team, *Expedition, Inc.,* to scope out the island chain and figure out where the pirates were operating from. Until now, the pirates had been doing an outstanding job of hiding themselves from the authorities. The island's natural topography went a long way toward the goal, high-tech camouflage filling in the difference.

"You know, that active camo netting is pretty impressive— for pirates, I mean," Scarlet said in Jason's and Sofia's ears.

"Please be careful, Jason," the team's resident archeologist and all-around science-guy Niles Kumalo pleaded.

"Don't worry, Doc. Like Scar said, most of the pirates are off chasing the decoy. Sofia and I will mark the buildings, take some recordings, and vamoose."

The older South African man made a noise Jason had learned was his polite disagreement noise.

"Yes, like that job in Singapore?" Sofia chuckled.

Jason looked at Sofia. She couldn't see his glare. "I've said it a thousand times, that spider was the size of a puppy and it startled me. Let it go."

Sofia held up a hand closed into a fist. Jason stopped dead in his tracks, head swiveling left and right, scanning. Sofia pointed with two fingers off to the right. Jason nodded.

Sofia Gomez had served in the United States Marine Corps for almost ten years. She'd fast tracked to Master Sergeant and would have continued on to much more had she not knocked her commanding officer out cold in front of several other enlisted. The audience had been a blessing and a curse; her superior officer had been making inappropriate gestures towards her and she had witnesses. Said witnesses were a curse because there was simply no way to brush the incident under the rug and move on, so she'd been given an assignment overseas where she would be out of the way.

Little did she know at the time, her assignment would lead to getting stuck in the middle of a firefight.

Aboard the *Raven*, Scarlet was in the Ops Center, Niles Kumalo standing over her shoulder. The Ops Center was in the heart of the *Raven*, connected to every comm system and sensor the craft had. The two of them were looking at several camera feeds from their decoy party barge. A vessel nearly fifty feet long had pulled alongside the barge. It didn't look like much, but the two forward-heavy machine guns with a pirate at the trigger made their intentions clear. Scarlet tapped the comm system. "Hey, Jace, you've got maybe twenty minutes, tops.

They're about to board the decoy, shouldn't take them long to clear it and high-tail it back here."

"Roger that," her boss replied.

JASON HAD CREPT UP TO WITHIN TEN FEET OF THE SENTRY. He glanced over to where Sofia was crouching near a sentry, two hundred feet further along the path toward the presumed pirate base of operations. The ex-marine nodded with her fist, bobbing it up and down, and both moved quickly to incapacitate their targets.

Jason looked at Sofia. "Let's get this done." They turned and made their way toward the camp quickly and quietly.

The camp was as deserted as they had expected. The pirate crew had left only a handful of people behind when the bulk of the group had gone out to raid the decoy vessel. Jason and Sofia had each crept around the opposite perimeter of the camp.

"Remember, the marker needs to be at least ten feet off the ground," Sofia reminded.

"Got it," Jason said, followed by a grunt as he climbed the tree he had chosen.

GETTING OUT IS THE HARD PART

SCARLET STARED AT ONE OF HER SCREENS, THEN TAPPED her earpiece. "Scratch that, Boss man. I think they're mad at being played. They're hauling nautical ass back to base. You've got like two minutes." An edge to her voice revealed how nervous she was. The *Raven* was holding position about a mile from shore off the southern tip of the island. Running quietly, she should be invisible to any sensors the pirates might have had.

"What?" Jason hissed. "You said twenty minutes five minutes ago."

Scarlet glanced at Niles, who shook his head slowly. "Yeah, well, now it's two. We can try to distract them with a drone or two," she offered.

"No," Jason said sharply. "We don't want to tip them off if we can avoid it. We've got two markers mounted. We'll get two more set up, then head for their dock. Bring the *Raven* around, but not too close. We may need to beat a hasty retreat."

"Roger that, Jace," Scarlet said, then moved her hand along a large track pad. She looked at one of the monitors overhead, an aerial view of the island chain, with an icon that represented the *Raven* in the center, a small blue smiley face. She dragged the smiley face to the approximate location Jason had indicated. She then looked at the ceiling. "Oracle, please power up, move us to the indicated location, maintain stealth."

"Acknowledged, moving to the selected location. Maintaining stealth," the speakers in the ceiling replied.

"I will never get used to how lifelike she is," Niles said, looking at the ceiling.

"She's a work of art, that's for sure," Scarlet answered, her eyes bright, pride showing across her freckled face.

JASON AND SOFIA PLACED THE LAST TWO MARKERS, JASON almost being discovered by a pirate that used the tree he was in as a toilet. From nearly twelve feet up, Jason watched the man take care of business, never once looking up. "I'm done and heading to you, Sof."

"Roger that. We should hurry. Guessing the bad guys on the boat called home. The two nearest me are pretty agitated." Her voice was tinny over the speaker in his tactical scuba helmet.

Jason dropped to the ground, careful to avoid the new wet patch at the base of the tree, and rushed off toward the icon that represented Sofia on his heads-up display. The base was quickly coming alive. Word of their compatriots' impending arrival was spreading.

"Hey, Scar, before I forget, power up the decoy and get it steaming for base. I hope the baddies didn't do anything that'll make us lose the deposit," Jason said as he worked his way quickly and quietly around the edge of the camp.

"They're docking," Niles reported over the comms as Jason

met up with Sofia. The two nodded to each other as they headed off into the jungle, following along beside a path that led to the dock where the pirate cutter was returning home.

Everything the Navy gave them before the mission had showed that the pirates, while a dangerous nuisance, were not that well equipped. That intel had been horribly wrong. The cutter was every bit as big and well armed as a US Coast Guard Cutter. It likely had started its life in the Coast Guard, Jason assumed. He couldn't be certain, but it looked like there was a small secondhand missile launcher mounted to an aft anchor point.

"Damn, these putas aren't messing around," Sofia whispered, clutching her FN P90 machine gun tightly against her torso, her free hand clenching and unclenching. She and Jason had ducked behind a large fallen tree a hundred or so feet from the dock. Between them and the dock was an open stretch of beach one hundred feet wide, dotted occasionally by a storage box or two.

Jason rested a hand on hers. "You're making me nervous. Cut it out," he said, smiling even though she couldn't see through his mirrored faceplate any more than he could see through hers. Tapping a control on his forearm, he zoomed in on the ship. "Twenty-two leaving. I'd assume at least one or two stay aboard at all times."

"All armed," Sofia added, noticing the AK-52s each man carried off the ship.

As the guards disembarked, four stopped and took up position at the shore side of the dock.

"Crap," Jason muttered. Two more men fell back about twenty feet from the first four, making six well-armed guards to get through before even getting aboard the cutter.

Sofia turned her mirrored faceplate toward Jason. "So?"

"So, we back off, get back to the *Raven*. This is too hot. We took care of part one. The Navy boys and girls can do the rest," Jason replied, slipping back away from the beach. Sofia grumbled something in Spanish and followed.

EVASIVE MANEUVERS

"I'm sending Huey and Duey your way. They can guide you," Scarlet said into the headset she was wearing.

The comms clicked twice, acknowledgement. Jason and Sofia kept silent.

The overhead speaker announced, "We have arrived at the designated location. I am disengaging engines and holding position."

A faint thunk sounded from somewhere overhead, the automated launching mechanism sending two mid-sized drones skyward. Each drone was matte black, and its running lights weren't lit. The sounds of their propellers were barely audible over the ocean waves.

Two of the many monitors in the Ops Center showed the view from each drone's camera. A block of green text in the upper corner of each display showed the name of the corresponding drone.

"What would you do if we had more than three drones?" Niles wondered from over Scarlet's shoulder.

"Easy: Fenton, Donald, Scrooge, Launchpad, Webby." She grinned up at the man. "Should I continue?"

He chuckled, "No, dear."

IN THE JUNGLE, BARELY A HALF A MILE FROM THE PIRATE cutter, Jason and Sofia quietly moved through the undergrowth. They had already retraced their steps twice to avoid patrols.

"These cabróns are well trained," Sofia said as two more pirates walked past her and Jason. They were crouched behind a rotten tree ten feet from the patrol. Their matte black dive suits blended in with the tall grass and shadows.

A light on both of their HUDs lit up. Jason looked up. "Our guides are here."

Sofia looked up, nodding. She made a motion with one hand, pointing toward the two waiting drones hovering offshore.

They'd gone ten yards when Jason tripped over something. His sealed helmet contained his yelp. Sofia leaned down to help him up, just as a bullet whizzed past to kick up a plume of sand.

"Shit!" Sofia cursed, dropping to her knee and spinning toward the direction the shot came from. "Nothing," she reported.

Jason rolled onto his stomach, bringing his compact machine gun to bear. "Move," he ordered.

Sofia crouched and dashed away from Jason so they could establish a better firing line.

"Contact, my ten," Jason said, his dark shape dropping into the tall grass to crawl a few feet away, just as bullets kicked up the sand where he was a moment before. "Tag him quick before his friends back him up."

Sofia peeked up over the grass, then ducked back down. She counted to three, then stood and fired a three-round burst. There was a short, muffled scream, then silence.

The two of them came together listening. Jason looked

around, waiting to see if anyone else arrived. In the distance, they heard shouting. He motioned to Sofia and headed toward the water at a trot.

Jason looked back toward the beach as he waded out into the ocean, his onboard HUD switching over to dive mode; a depth gauge appeared in the bottom left corner of his vision. His current oxygen level popped up in the top right. As he sank lower, he saw a dozen armed men rush to the beach, looking all around, flashlight beams playing across the sand and the water. His head dipped below the surface.

The swim back to the *Raven* took almost an hour, during which Jason and Sofia had to stop and wait for small patrol boats to pass only three times, keeping themselves ten feet below the surface as the boats passed nearby.

CHESS AND ENCHILADAS

BACK ABOARD THE *RAVEN*, JASON AND SOFIA STRIPPED OFF their tactical scuba gear, leaving just their swimsuits underneath. Scarlet and Niles were waiting for them just outside the changing room of the *Raven's* moon pool in the forward section of the boat. Scarlet looked from the monitor set next to the hatch to Niles. "Won't lie, that view never gets old."

The heavy-set archeologist grunted, "Which view?" His eyes didn't leave the display.

"Either," the hacker said, then wheeled over to the hatch leading deeper inside the ship. She waved a hand. "Come on."

Niles harrumphed and followed her out, waving a hand over his head at Jason and Sofia as they exited the room following him.

Scarlet was the first to arrive in the Ops Center. As the last of the team entered, she turned. "Okay, so the markers and cameras are all five by five. General Hearnan's office confirmed the feeds. We got paid, people!" She rolled over to high five Jason, who returned the gesture with gusto before heading to the small table in the room's corner. He slid next to Niles, followed by Sofia.

Jason looked over at the many displays mounted around the lowered desk, just the right height for Scarlet's chair, and nodded. "Okay, cool. Let's get underway." He looked at the ceiling. "Oracle, please set a course for home, half speed."

"Acknowledged, course set for home, half speed," the feminine voice replied from semi-hidden speakers in the ceiling. From somewhere further aft, the sound of the massive engines powering up rumbled through the hull. Then the slight lurch of movement followed.

Jason looked to Sofia. "I believe it's your turn to cook dinner?"

The lean-muscled woman nodded. "Yeah, let me go change, sí? I'm thinking enchiladas." She slid out of the booth and walked toward the exit of the Ops Center.

Jason nodded. "Yeah, I should get out of these trunks, too. See everyone in the mess." He got up from the table and followed Sofia out.

Niles and Scarlet looked at each other, then headed for the main living space one deck up from the Ops Center. The *Raven* was a converted luxury yacht that Jason had picked up at a state auction. The previous owner had been a high-level agent in one of the South American cartels, and the boat, called the *Guadalupe* then, had been his base of operations. The living spaces were luxurious but not over the top, while the technical sections were state-of-the art, including the moon pool and a small boat launch facility, not to mention the computer center and other spaces.

As Sofia set about prepping dinner, Jason and Niles set up a chess game, while Scarlet busied herself with her laptop at the dinner table.

Jason moved one of his pawns. "Excellent move, Jason," Niles complimented before moving one of his bishops to seize the just-moved pawn. The older South African man smiled, his teeth standing out brightly against his jet-black skin.

Jason groaned, moving another piece, a knight.

"So, Jason, can we talk about our next assignment?" Niles pressed. He had asked the same question every other night since they had accepted the job to identify the pirate stronghold and, if possible, disable their craft. They'd succeeded in the former, but the latter had proven more difficult than expected. Niles moved a knight, grinned, then looked up at his friend and employer.

Jason sighed. "Yes, Niles, we can. I assume you have something in mind?" Jason picked up another pawn, moved it, then rested a finger on it until he was certain it was the move he wanted to make. He lifted his finger and made eye contact with Niles.

The older man nodded. "In fact, I do. I have been monitoring several of the academic bulletin boards. There are several university-backed projects that could use this team's unique skill sets." He picked up one of his own pawns, moving it in next to the one Jason just moved.

"Sounds boring," Scarlet said from the other side of the kitchen table where she had wheeled up to, her laptop balanced precariously on a dinner plate. "I bet I could find something juicy, hostage rescue or stealing an ancient artifact from a Soviet oligarch. You know, something exciting." She peeked over the top of her laptop, eyebrows arched.

Niles harrumphed, raising a hand. "This last assignment was of the danger-close variety. I believe it is my turn to have a say in the job. Correct?" He glanced back to Jason.

Jason nodded. "Yup, Doc is right. We just did the action

adventure thing. It's his turn to flex his muscles on a job." He glanced at over to the older, heavier-set man. "Figuratively," he winked.

Niles deftly picked up a knight, moving it. "Check." His own black-haired eyebrow raised.

TWO

SIDE PROJECTS

Before joining *Expedition, Inc.*, Scarlet Jones was a successful and highly-in-demand computer programmer. She graduated from the Massachusetts Institute of Technology when she was fifteen. Her prospects were bright—until the accident, the accident that put her in a wheelchair. She was still every bit as in demand from Fortune 10 companies after the accident but had lost all interest in the hacker-for-hire game.

A distracted driver, busy with her phone, jumped the curb outside a bookstore in downtown Los Angeles. Scarlet lost three friends and was paralyzed from the waist down. During her months of recovery and subsequent months of enforced isolation, she created Oracle, the most advanced artificial intelligence ever created, as far as Scarlet knew. Oracle was a closely guarded secret. She had only told Jason about the AI after he'd hired her and she knew he wouldn't try to market or otherwise exploit Scarlet's work.

"Scarlet, we're about ten minutes from home," Oracle said from the speaker in the ceiling of Scarlet's berth.

Scarlet looked up from her workstation, soldering iron,

weaving a stream of smoke. "Thanks, Oracle. Please let Jason know. He likes to be the one to park."

"Of course. I've already notified him," the ever-cheerful computer replied.

Scarlet pushed away from her desk, turned her chair, and rolled toward the door to her quarters and the corridor beyond.

After the accident she had tried for years to create a technological solution to her paralysis. When the solution to that particular problem continued to elude her she did the next best thing, in her mind. She created a series of more and more complex and functional wheelchairs. She was currently sitting in what she called the Mark ten.

ON THE BRIDGE OF THE *RAVEN*, JASON KINCAID WORKED the controls, bringing the converted mega yacht into its slip at a high end and very private marina just north of Sea World in San Diego, California.

"Well done, Jason," Oracle said from the speaker in the steering console in the center of the high-tech bridge.

"Thanks, O," Jason said, powering down the engines and flipping switches to put the boat's systems into standby mode. As he headed out of the bridge, he turned back. "Hey, O, have everyone meet up at the boarding ramp." Automated arms reached out from the dock and grasped specially designed hard points along the length of the ship to keep her in place.

"Acknowledged—all crew meet at the boarding ramp," the speaker replied, the last part of the sentence coming from every speaker on the boat.

By the time Jason made his way three levels down to the heavy hatch on the side of the *Raven*, the others were waiting. He looked around. "Okay, it's late. We'll get the boat unpacked in the morning and figure out our next move then. Sound good?" Nods all around. He turned and walked down the ramp. "'Night, all."

Scarlet followed, guiding her chair down the ramp. She tapped a button on the arm of the chair. "Oracle, lock the boat down, please."

"Acknowledged, locking down the *Raven*," the small speaker built into the back of her chair responded.

As everyone headed off into the building, Scarlet rolled toward one of the outbuildings near the dock. She tapped a few keys on the panel at her arm, and the door ahead opened automatically.

"Good evening, Scarlet," Oracle said as the lights came on, followed by several monitors and the faint hum of computer fans spinning up.

She wheeled over to a specially modified desk, just the right height for someone in a wheelchair like hers. A few taps of the keyboard and everything around her sprung to life.

"Okay, Oracle, let's get cracking. How are the simulations of version five coming?"

One of the larger displays switched to a wire frame of an aircraft appeared. "Version five is performing well within expected parameters and out-performing the previous four versions by an average of twenty-two percent."

Scarlet pumped her fist in the air. "Yes!" She spun her chair once then rolled over to a large computer-assisted drawing tablet. "Bring up the power plant schematics, please." The tablet screen brightened and a full set of schematics appeared. Scarlet picked up the pen and started making adjustments.

HOME SWEET HOME

THE *EXPEDITION, INC.,* BUILDING WAS A FIVE-STORY converted office building in a mostly abandoned office park. Jason bought it years ago after his first successful deep-water salvage. The ruins of a Viking longship off the coast of Washington State not only proved that their range was much greater than originally thought, but the hold full of valuable artifacts had set Jason and *Expedition, Inc.,* up for the first few years.

After that, it wasn't hard to assemble a small team of experts and find clients in need of their unique skills. Having direct and private access to the small marina where the *Raven* sat was a bonus.

The smell of freshly brewed coffee and frying eggs worked its way up to the fifth floor, the floor Jason kept for himself: living space, workout area, and workshop. The freight elevator worked its way slowly up, while Jason checked his email on his phone.

When the door opened, Jason walked in, bumping into the substantially heavier Niles. "Oof," Jason grunted, almost falling backwards until the South African scientist grabbed his arm, keeping him upright.

"Sorry, Jason!" He righted the younger man. "Sofia sent me to fetch you."

"She hates it when people are late to a meal," Jason said, nodding as he joined the African man in the elevator. He punched the button for *one*.

"I ALMOST ATE YOURS," SCARLET SAID AS THE ELEVATOR doors opened, releasing Jason and Niles.

"It'd go to your hips," Jason quipped, quickly dodging an airborne piece of bacon.

Niles tutted, "My dear! Crimes against bacon!"

"Sorry, Doc, my girlish figure demanded defending," Scarlet grinned, popping a piece of bacon into her mouth.

Sofia walked over from the fully stocked chef's kitchen that Jason had had installed just for her after she joined the team two years ago, holding a frying pan with two sizzling eggs in it. "Late night?"

Jason nodded. "Yeah, was going over the data with Major Thompson. He wasn't thrilled that we didn't disable their cutter." He took a bite of eggs. "Excellent as always, Sof. He did a lot of stomping around and fuming, but the data stream from the markers was enough for him to call in a strike, so end of the day, good guys one, bad guys no longer on the board." He grinned and took another bite. "At any rate, he's happy. So is the General, so you know that's good."

Niles nodded while taking his own seat at the table. "So, then, with that assignment officially closed out, I have a proposal for the team." He looked around to make sure he had everyone's attention. Niles had been a college professor prior to Jason hiring him on full time. Before that he had been a moderately famous archeologist and anthropologist, until his indiscretions with an assistant came to light.

She was of legal age and consenting, but that didn't stop the financial backers of his projects from insisting he leave all projects or they'd pull their funding, the University overseeing the projects took no time in showing him the door. The assistant's wealthy parents had made quick work of the man they viewed as a predator.

He considered himself lucky to get the teaching job after that, toiling in semi-obscurity hoping to retire with tenure. Once he was certain his silence had brought all eyes to him, he continued, "An old friend of mine has found herself with what could be a major discovery. She needs a team to help get her there and do the work."

"That's some next level, kung fu master level of crypticness," Scarlet said, taking a bite of her eggs after running her fork through some syrup from her waffles.

"That's gross," Jason said, watching her.

She made a face and Niles cleared his throat. "Well, yes, unfortunately she wasn't willing to elaborate until we accept the job."

"She can pay?" Jason asked, eyebrow raised. Niles loved taking pro-bono work, even though no one else did.

"Of course she can, Jason. Her university, while not willing to devote manpower to her quest, has agreed to fund it." He shifted his glance. "At least mostly."

"Mostly?" Jason asked.

"Why is her school unwilling to devote the manpower?" Sofia asked, coming to the table, her own plate heaped with eggs, waffles, and bacon. She slapped Jason's hand when he reached for a piece of her bacon before taking a seat next to him.

Niles glanced away. "Well, they deemed the expedition too dangerous to risk their own students, faculty, or equipment."

"And there we go," Scarlet said.

"I like danger," Sofia said before shoving a forkful of eggs into her mouth.

UPGRADES

"I mean, it sounds like an *US* job," Jason said, looking at his friend. The South African man finally glanced over and grinned. Jason held up a hand. "Set up a meeting. You know the rules."

Niles' head bobbed like a dashboard decoration. "Of course, of course." He stood up. "I'll see to it right away."

"You know, when he's this excited about a job, it worries me," Sofia said, watching the heavyset anthropologist rush toward the communications nook set in the building's corner.

Jason looked over to her. "Eat your breakfast. We've got to get the *Raven* cleaned up and serviced before we take any new gigs." Sofia nodded, shoving a mouthful of egg and waffle into her mouth, grinning around it. "You're all disgusting," Jason huffed, shoving himself off the bench he and Sofia were sharing.

"How's your pet project coming along?" Jason asked Scarlet as they moved about the ready room aboard the *Raven*, tidying up.

Scarlet rolled over to one of the storage lockers. "How does this boat get disgusting in such a short time?" She dropped her armload of maps and charts into the locker. "We were only at sea for a week."

Jason picked up a rifle, mumbling something about Sofia and toys. He looked at his friend and team hacker. "It is pretty amazing how quickly this place gets messy. You're avoiding the question," he grinned.

Scarlet spun. "I am. It's coming along. That industrial 3D printer is a godsend." She rolled toward the hatch. "But it'll still be a while. Have you heard about the delivery?"

Jason nodded. "Yeah, I'm guessing it'll arrive while we're doing whatever it is Niles' friend needs. Assuming we leave in the next day or so." He smiled, following her out. "Look at it this way. You'll have something to look forward to."

They entered the small elevator, specially designed and added to the boat after Jason hired Scarlet. "And how's Oracle doing?"

"I am right here, you know?" the ceiling of the elevator said.

Jason laughed. "Fair enough. You did well during that last job, Oracle. The *Raven's* upgrades seem to agree with you."

The elevator doors opened. Jason extended his arm, ushering Scarlet out onto the bridge of the *Raven*. The wheeled hacker looked up. "Yeah, that new computing core was just what she needed. The local area network held up much better this time."

"It did, Scarlet. I did not mention it at the time, but I lost connection to the moon pool deck briefly while engaging the engines to move the *Raven*. One of the mesh nodes dropped out but returned."

Scarlet scratched her chin. "Oh, good to know. Send me a note with which node, and I'll look." She looked over to Jason, who had busied himself at the command station. "Do you think we'll be taking the *Raven* on Niles' job?"

Jason shrugged. "No idea."

Scarlet spun and rolled toward one of the other computer terminals. "Okay then, Oracle, let's make sure you're travel ready." She turned to Jason. "That high-gain antenna was a great addition. She can hop between the building, my workshop, and the *Raven* with almost no lag."

Jason nodded.

"JASON, THIS IS MY FRIEND ASAKO. ASAKO YAMAMOTO OF the University of British Columbia Asian studies department." Niles and a stunning Japanese woman walked into the conference room on the first floor of the *Expedition, Inc.*, building two days later.

Asako approached Jason, hand extended. "It's a pleasure to meet you in person, Mr. Kincaid. I've been an admirer for many years. Your career is something of a legend in a lot of universities."

Jason shook the offered hand, then gestured for Yamamoto and Niles to sit. "I'm a little surprised my exploits reach the cultural studies folks. Not exactly an area we do a lot of work in, at least not directly."

Asako smiled. "Universities are small places. The anthropology and archeology folks often share lunch with us culture nerds." She chuckled. "Strength in numbers when the hard sciences folks show up."

Jason nodded. "Fair enough." He leaned forward on the table. "So, why don't you tell me what you need my team and I for?"

The petite woman bowed. "To put it simply, I've discovered... something." She held up a small hand, forcing Jason to swallow the question he was about to ask. "I wish I knew more, but until I'm there, I just don't. If I'm right, it could be one of those *discoveries-of-a-lifetime*-type of things."

"Still not many details..." Jason pressed.

Asako leaned forward. "I believe I may have found a secret Japanese World War Two base in Canada."

Jason leaned back. "Well, damn."

THREE

NEW JOB

"Everyone, this is Asako Yamamoto, our client," Jason said as he exited the elevator on the second floor. The second floor of the building was where *Expedition, Inc.,* kept their business offices and a large conference room.

Scarlet rolled over. "Hi, I'm Scarlet, the smart one." She gestured toward an ornate set of double doors at the end of a hallway.

Asako bowed slightly. "A pleasure. All groups need a smart woman."

Scarlet grinned and offered a fist that Asako dutifully bumped her own against.

Sofia looked up from the magazine she was reading. "Hey." Asako nodded. Everyone headed into the conference room.

Niles walked over to a large display with a keyboard and track pad mounted next to it at the end of the long room. He punched a few keys, then the screen lit up. He nodded to Jason.

Jason cleared his throat. "Here's the deal." He looked over to Scarlet, who had rolled over next to Sofia at the side of the table near where Jason was sitting at the head. Niles and Asako took seats opposite the team's weapons expert. "I was wrong. We'll need the *Raven*. We'll sail up the coast into Canada. Ms. Yamamoto works at the University of British Columbia, and so we'll be stopping there to re-supply. As Niles mentioned earlier, the University is not interested in sending any of their people but will pay for us to go on what they believe to be a dangerous wild goose chase. While they're not willing to risk their people, they don't want to risk losing out if it turns out Ms. Yamamoto is correct."

Sofia grunted, "So, what? We're going to Canada, to what? Look for sea monsters? There's an airport in Vancouver, near the University, if I recall. Faster to fly."

Jason nodded. "You're right, flying would be much faster, but after we stop at the University, we'll be continuing north to Graham Island." He held a hand up. "No sea monsters." He glanced at Asako, who shook her head, then worriedly looked at Niles, who shook his head. "But the *Raven* will be our FOB for this job, it looks like."

"How far north? Cold weather gear?" Sofia asked.

Niles worked the computer, adjusting the screen to show Graham Island. "Not that far north. This time of year, we should be okay with regular gear."

Asako nodded, adding, "Correct, while not as warm as here, it is by no means cold right now in that area."

Sofia looked at Jason. "So, what're we doing?"

Jason looked at Niles and then Asako. "Would you like to do the honors?"

Asako stood and walked over to the wall-mounted display, adjusting the image a bit. "My field of study is mid-twentieth century Japanese culture, specifically the years around World War Two. While reviewing some recently released documents from the Japanese ministry of defense, I realized something."

"And?" Sofia made a *go on* motion with her hand.

Asako blushed slightly. "Yes, well, I believe I've found evidence of a secret Japanese research base on Graham Island."

Scarlet leaned forward in her chair, then raised a hand. "If the Ministry of Defense released the documents, wouldn't they know that it revealed this base? And if so, wouldn't that mean either: the base, if it exists, is cleaned out, or that there isn't a base?"

Asako nodded, smiling. "You are quite right, Ms. Scarlet; however, the documents do not at all mention a base. The Ministry, in an effort to shed light on those years, released thousands of pages of information, from run-of-the-mill daily status reports to acquisition requests. Taken individually, nothing they released would make one think there is a base in Canada. However, taken in their entirety, the evidence becomes clearer. Not crystal clear, but patterns emerged. Acquisition requests for certain project names, shipping manifests, even those routine daily status reports, all add up." She was beaming now. "I do not believe anyone in the Ministry now even knows or suspects such a base might exist."

"So, why not go to the Japanese?" Jason asked, tapping his foot.

"Oh, I did. Much like the University, they discounted the idea as ridiculous."

"I mean, it kinda is," Sofia said, leaning back in the sofa, her feet on the coffee table.

"You are right, it is, but the evidence is right here." She pointed to the screen, and Jason jumped to move the image of the map to the side, showing hundreds of folders of information. Asako added, "And while the University does not see the value in sending any of their people—

outside myself, of course—and I'm taking a leave of absence, they will help provision an expedition. Hedging their bets, as you say."

GETTING UNDERWAY

"THESE WILL BE YOUR QUARTERS WHILE YOU'RE WITH US," Jason said as he opened the door to the normally unused guest quarters on the *Raven*. The two walked in and Jason spun slowly, taking in the moderately sized room. "That door is a shared restroom with the berth next to yours, but it's empty, so pretty much all yours." He pointed to ceiling. "If you need anything, just ask Oracle. If you need one of us, she can connect you."

Asako looked at the ceiling. "Who is *Oracle*?"

"I am," the ceiling answered. "I am the team's fifth member."

Jason groaned under his breath. "She can be a bit theatrical. Oracle is an experimental artificial intelligence created by Scarlet. She manages several of the *Raven's* systems for us." He pointed at the ceiling again. "She's always listening unless you explicitly tell her to activate privacy mode."

Asako looked around the room, then back to the ceiling. "Can she see us?"

Jason opened his mouth to answer, but Oracle beat him to it. "I cannot, Ms. Yamamoto. The *Raven* only has cameras in the mission-specific areas of the ship, such as the Ops Center and bridge, or common areas like the corridors and lounge."

Asako let out an appreciative whistle. "I knew Ms. Jones was smart but did not realize she was *that* kind of smart."

Jason had a knowing grin on his face. "You have no idea, but she doesn't like to brag and hates it when we do, so she's our best kept secret."

"Indeed." She looked at the ceiling one more time. "Well, Oracle, it is my honor to meet you." She bowed slightly.

"The honor is mine, Ms. Yamamoto, yōkoso," Oracle replied.

Jason looked at the Japanese woman, one eyebrow quirked.

"You may call me Asako, and your Japanese is excellent. Yoku yatta."

Jason turned toward the door. "I'll leave you two to chat and unpack. If you need anything, just ask." He pointed at the ceiling again to emphasize.

Jason found Niles helping Scarlet in the computer bay. "Hey, you two, anything I need to worry about? Thinking we shove off in an hour, we can welcome our client-slash-guest with dinner. Thinking Chinese delivery since we'll be at sea for a few days. This is our last chance until Vancouver to get anything other than what's in the reefer."

The hacker and archeologist both looked up. Niles replied, "Chinese sounds wonderful. Wu-Tang's?"

"Of course."

Scarlet pointed toward one of the many server racks in the space. "I'd like to get a new satellite comms module. Not mission critical, but the one we've got is pretty old." Her eyebrows raised at Jason. "And we're lacking more modern encryption options and such. This one is okay, but limited. Also," she pointed to another rack, "we should invest in a few more GPUs for that rack. It'll really speed Oracle up."

"I feel like I should take offense," the speaker in the ceiling said.

"You don't have feelings. But don't worry. I love you like you are, but there's always room for improvement," Scarlet said as she looked up at the speaker.

"It is very disconcerting when you two banter," Niles said, looking from his wheelchair-bound friend to the ceiling. "No offense meant, my digital love."

The speaker made a tutting noise but offered nothing else.

"Okay, then. I'll leave you three to whatever you were doing. I'll get grub ordered. We shove off at sixteen." Jason turned and left the well-cooled room, closing the door behind him.

"I forget how antsy he gets before a job starts," Niles said, looking at the closed door.

Scarlet shrugged. "He can be tightly wound sometimes. Meh."

SET SAIL

"Oracle, make sure you lock the building up, and please set the out of office," Scarlet said as the *Raven's* engines rumbled to life. Everyone was on the bridge as the large luxury-yacht-turned-mobile-command-center backed out of her slip.

"The building is locked up tight, like always," the company's artificial intelligence replied.

"Good girl, thank you," Scarlet replied. She turned to Jason. "Let's get this show on the road."

The *Raven* finished backing out her slip and slowly turned, bringing her nose toward the exit of the marina and the ocean beyond.

Jason spent some time guiding the vessel out of the marina and out into the ocean. Once they were miles from the office and a steady two miles from the shoreline, he turned in his chair to look around the small bridge. Scarlet and Sofia left shortly after they departed. Only Niles remained. "Ready for dinner, old man?" He smiled.

"Indeed, I am, Captain." The older South African man stood and turned to the exit hatch.

Jason looked up to the ceiling. "Oracle, please take over the conn and keep us on course."

"Of course, Jason."

"Gods, I love Wu-Tang's," Sofia said, reaching across the table and spearing an egg roll with a single chopstick.

Asako watched with interest. "Impressive."

Jason spooned up a mass of kung pao chicken. "Our Sofia here is an ex-marine."

Sofia took a bite of her egg roll, still on the end of a chopstick, and smiled. After finishing her bite, she added, "Honorably discharged. I served ten years, mostly overseas. Took a few rounds to the middle. When I woke, I left." She ate the last of the egg roll on her chopstick. "Jason found me after I got fired from my first job out of the service."

Jason finished chewing. "She broke three coworkers' jaws."

Asako's eyes went wide. "I hope they deserved it."

Sofia grinned. "I like her, and yes, they very much did." She reached past Niles to grab the last of a bowl of orange chicken.

Jason offered, "She was working for a private security firm. A client of mine had hired them for muscle on a job and Sofia impressed me."

Scarlet waved away the rest of the story Jason was about to tell and rested her elbows on the table, leaning forward looking at Asako. "So, tell us more about this base you think you've found."

Asako grabbed a wonton off the platter in the middle of the table, setting it on her plate. "We all know how active the Japanese were in the Pacific theater." She looked around at the nodding heads. "Everything we've ever come across told us they prowled mostly around the western coast of the United States, which makes sense. Outside of the battle of Saint Lawrence, most of Canada's participation in World War Two was across the ocean in Europe."

Niles slid his plate toward the center of the table. "You mentioned records recently made public?"

Asako continued, "Right, yes. The Japanese government over the last ten or more years has been slowly releasing more and more documents from that time period, mostly for posterity and to help ease our cultural conscience in showing what our military and government were up to." She took a sip of her water, then added, "Part of my research has been to catalog all of this data into a more searchable format. I stumbled across the clues to the base entirely by accident. As I was going through the various pieces of documentation, I saw patterns emerging." She looked around, realizing that everyone had stopped eating to listen to her story. "And, well, here we are."

<h1 style="text-align:center; letter-spacing:0.2em;">BACK TO SCHOOL</h1>

"Welcome to Wreck Beach," Asako said as the *Raven* slowly maneuvered into a slip at the University of British Columbia docks, a relatively new addition to the school's property, replacing a small beach that few students used after a grisly accident several years prior.

The rumble of the *Raven's* engines quieted, then came to a stop completely, the large vessel rocking slightly against the dock.

There was another boat docked nearby, the name and registration missing. "Wonder who that is?" Jason asked as he secured the controls, glancing out the bridge windows at the mysterious vessel.

Asako and Niles followed his gaze, the latter shrugging, the former offering, "Must belong to the University. No one else really uses this dock, as far as I know."

Jason got up and walked toward the hatch. He looked over to Asako. "So, what now?"

The Asian woman shook her head. "My office. My research is there, and assuming my assistants did their job, the supplies I requested should be there, too."

Jason opened the bridge hatch, extending his arm. "Lead the way." He looked over to Scarlet. "Why don't you stay here and see what kind of computer-y trouble you can get into." He winked.

Scarlet followed Jason and Asako out of the bridge, followed by Niles. The red-haired hacker turned the opposite direction everyone else did, heading for the elevator. "I'll be on comms in a minute." Niles nodded as he followed Jason and Asako down the stairs.

As Scarlet rolled into the Ops Center, the lights came on followed by the many monitors around the space. The specially designed station that Scarlet worked from came alive, desk segments shifting as she rolled into position. Once the final component clicked into place, touch screen displays and keyboards nearly surrounded her. "Time to get to work, Oracle," she said, smiling at the main display of the workstation, currently showing a wireframe diagram of the *Raven*.

"Hello, Scarlet. That's exciting. What should we do first?" While there were speakers in the ceiling for Oracle to use, when it was just Scarlet in the room, the AI used one of the displays with a speaker embedded behind the glass. A colorful display shifted and adjusted as the AI spoke.

"Full network infiltration," the hacker replied.

"Oh, it's that kind of job?" the computer intelligence asked, her synthesized voice an octave higher than normal, her equivalent of laughter.

Scarlet tapped the main keyboard for a minute, then pressed a finger to her ear activating the small comm unit there. "I'm almost in. I'll keep you posted. Holler if you need anything."

"Roger that, Overwatch," Jason replied, using the codename the team had adopted for the hacker when they were on the job.

"Scarlet, I have detected several firewalls, presumably departmental. Do we want to breach each of them?"

"Yeah, I don't think we need to, exactly, but better safe than sorry. We should only be here a day at the most, so let's not make a mess."

"Of course. No one will know we've been here," Oracle replied.

"THIS WAY." ASAKO POINTED TOWARD A LOW BUILDING with a pyramid-shaped roof at the end of the street they had found themselves on upon following University Boulevard from the marina entry. She turned left down the street toward the building. She looked back. "With school being out, there aren't many students on campus other than the summer semester kids. After we retrieve the data and supplies, we should grab dinner. The Pit Pub makes a good poutine."

"I love a good poutine," Niles said, rubbing his rather substantial stomach.

Sofia quirked an eyebrow. "Oh, do you?" The portly African man blushed, his already dark skin turning a shade or two darker still.

"Job, then dinner," Jason said, his head turning from side to side.

FOUR

FIRE THE CLEANING SERVICE

As far as Jason and the team could tell, the Asian Centre building was deserted. The few lights on seemed to have been left on from earlier that day or possibly a different day altogether. With the school in summer session, only a fraction of faculty and students were on campus.

Asako used her keycard to open the doors. "My office is downstairs. We can take the stairs; the elevator is notoriously slow."

Niles looked around. "How many levels does this building have? It appeared to be one story from the outside."

"Only three; this floor is mostly lecture halls and other classrooms. The two floors below are faculty offices and the like. We've been promised a new building for, oh, this is the ninth year, if I recall correctly." The petite Asian woman shrugged and headed down the stairs.

Sofia was the last to exit the stairwell. "This isn't spooky," she whispered. For emphasis, she ran a finger along Niles' neck, causing him to make a yipe-like noise.

Asako and Jason tried their best to stifle their laughter.

When they came to a stop, Asako looked back at Jason. "I closed this when I left the other day."

Jason put a hand on her shoulder, guiding her away from the door, while simultaneously motioning for Sofia to come forward. In a whisper he asked, "When were you here last? Would your assistants have left it open?"

Asako pressed a finger to her lips. "I guess about six or seven days ago now. After I heard from Niles, I went home and packed, then flew down to your office." She shook her head. "It's possible, but they know better."

Sofia moved up to the side of the door, her hand resting on the handle. In her other hand, a pistol. She mouthed the words, *three, two, one*, then pushed open the door and rushed in. A few seconds passed, then, "Clear."

Jason entered, followed by Asako and Niles. He whistled, "Wow, you do not keep a tidy workplace."

The Asian woman pushed past Jason, making a rude noise. "Someone has trashed my office!"

Niles entered last, looking around the room. "Oh my."

"Who? Why?" Asako stammered.

"You said you told the Japanese government. Anyone else?" Jason walked over to Asako's desk and the remains of her computer.

"Why would the Japanese do this? I offered them the data. Why trash my office?"

Sofia came over to the desk. "Wasn't the Japanese." When everyone stared at her expectantly, she added, "Too messy. If they had wanted the data, they'd have just taken the computer or hacked in."

Jason nodded. "Agree. I think it was someone else." He looked at Asako again, eyebrow raised.

Before she could answer, Scarlet said, "Uh, I might at least have some additional information to add."

"Go ahead, Overwatch," Jason said.

"Someone else has been in this network. We haven't figured out who yet, but we're working on it."

"Okay, that's interesting. Thanks, Overwatch." Jason turned back to Asako. "Who else?"

Asako tapped her chin, thinking. "I mean, I mentioned it to my colleague Martin. He's a professor in the Chemical and--"

"Chemical and Bioengineering department?" Scarlet interrupted over the comms, forcing Jason to hold up his hand to stop Asako.

Jason repeated what Scarlet had said.

Asako nodded. "Yes, how did she know?"

Scarlet said, "Oracle and I have isolated the compromised servers. They're in the Chem and Bioengineering department." Jason repeated what she said, then she added, "I'm guessing her friend made a note or sent an email or something. Who knows? I could probably find it, but that's beside the point at this stage." Again, Jason repeated back the report. "We haven't figured out who hacked the servers yet, but clearly someone was hoping for some biochem secrets and got World War Two secrets instead."

After Jason repeated the latest, Asako grunted, "At least my theory is pretty much confirmed."

Niles cocked his head. "One way to look at it."

Sofia looked around again. "Uh, so now what?" She nodded toward the desk and the ruined computer on its surface. "Guessing we won't be getting your notes and whatnot from *that.*"

ALWAYS HAVE A BACKUP

"Does Ms. Jones have access to the servers for this department?" Asako asked.

Scarlet tutted. "Of course I do, tell her of course I do," she instructed.

Jason nodded. "She does."

Asako looked around. "Then let's gather up what we can and get back to your boat. I can show Scarlet where my backups are. I can't imagine whoever did this got to those."

Niles looked at the room. "We can still get dinner first, right?"

Jason groaned. "Yeah, might as well. We've got a few days of sailing ahead of us. Overwatch, put the *Raven* on lockdown and meet us up here. I'll send Sofia to get you." He looked over to the Hispanic woman, who nodded and left the ransacked office. He looked over to Asako. "Do you have any idea which of these they meant to come with us?"

She pointed to several boxes. "Those. They weren't here when I left." She turned toward the far side of the room. "I should check on my assistants." She pulled her phone out of her pocket and moved it to her ear as she stepped out into the hall.

Niles walked over to Jason as the younger man bent down to inspect the boxes left by Asako's assistants. "Jason, something is afoot."

Jason looked at his friend. "You don't say, Watson, what could it be?" he asked in his best British accent.

Niles crossed his arms. "Jason, this is serious. Someone clearly thinks Asako has found something."

Jason stood, holding one of the boxes. "Won't be the first time we've been in a race, Niles, or the last. Scarlet will work her magic and we'll see who we're dealing with. Then we'll adjust." He grinned his best reassuring smile. "When has a job ever been a cakewalk?"

Niles looked at one of the other boxes. "I suppose so, though there was that job in Egypt. That was a cakewalk."

Jason laughed. "Well, yeah, that was an easy one." He nodded towards the box Niles was eyeing. "Exception, definitely not the rule."

"Oracle, you heard the man, secure the ship. I'll wait for Sofia on the dock."

The workstation began shifting to allow for Scarlet to roll out of the alcove. "Of course, Scarlet, once you depart, I will lock up the *Raven*."

Scarlet rolled out of the Ops Center toward the small elevator in the center of the boat. The loading deck was one level down from the Ops Center. The massive watertight door stood open; a deployable ramp extended to the dock a few feet lower than the door. As Scarlet rolled through the door, she looked over a shoulder. "I'm out, lock her up. See you soon."

"Enjoy dinner," the AI replied over the commset in Scarlet's ear.

Up ahead, Sofia was walking down the long, raised sidewalk connecting the dock to the mainland.

Scarlet began rolling toward the ramp and her friend. "Did you run here?"

"Why walk when you can run?" the athletic woman grinned. "Ready for chow?"

"Damn right," Scarlet replied, rolling past her friend up the walkway. She looked over her shoulder. "Since you like to run, keep up." She pushed the control on her chair forward, driving her speed up. She rocketed away from Sofia.

"Damn chica!" the ex-marine grunted as she jumped into a comfortable run to catch up with her friend. Her friend laughed. "Uh, you know where to go, yeah?"

Scarlet held up a data pad with her free hand. On it was a map of the campus.

"Cheeky," Sofia panted.

"Oh, Asako, this place brings back memories," Niles said, putting down a half empty pint glass of lager.

Scarlet looked up at the African archeologist. "I didn't know you taught here?"

Niles shook his head, "Oh no, dear, I didn't, but surely even the ivy-covered halls of MIT had a bar similar to this? Every school I've ever been to has had a pub like this."

Scarlet deadpanned a look at the man. "I was underage, and you know," she motioned to the chair, "not really into the party scene."

Niles blushed. "Oh."

Asako put a hand on his arm, keeping him from saying anything else.

Jason looked at Niles, then Scarlet. "You fall for shit every time."

Scarlet snorted, wiggling her eyebrows. "You're such an easy mark, Niles. Of course MIT had a bar like this!" she laughed. "I was still underage, though, so you know." She turned serious, pulling her tablet out of the pouch on her chair. "Okay, Asako, let's get your data. You said you had it backed up somewhere?" She tapped a few commands into her tablet, then handed it across the table.

As Asako reached for the tablet, the waiter came over with two large baskets, one full of chicken wings, the other steaming poutine. She adjusted her reach to avoid the nearest basket and caught the eye of the waiter. "Oh, you must be new. Working the summer term?"

"Uh, yeah. Yeah, the summer term." He set the baskets down and departed.

Jason quirked an eyebrow.

Asako looked at the tablet, tapping something on screen. "Oh, here it is. Thank God." She tapped the screen a few times, then handed the device back to Scarlet.

Sofia grabbed a wing, putting the whole thing in her mouth, removing a meatless bone a moment later.

Niles made a noise. "That is a truly disturbing skill, Sofia." The Hispanic woman grinned and winked.

Scarlet looked up. "Okay, all of Asako's data is on the *Raven*. To be safe, Oracle will upload it to our secure cloud, as well."

OBVIOUS GUY IS OBVIOUS

Halfway through their beers, one entire basket of wings later, Sofia looked at Jason. "Something is wrong."

"Like existentially or..." he replied.

She looked at everyone, then tilted her head sideways. "Our *waiter* hasn't taken his eyes off us since we got here." She looked at Asako. "You didn't recognize him, right?"

Asako glanced over to the waiter who had brought their food. He was standing near the bar, trying to not look like he was watching them. "That is correct, but that doesn't mean much. It's not like I know everyone who works here. They're students usually, and they come and go with the semesters."

"He seems to be intentionally obvious, or is it just me?" Scarlet said glancing over at the probably not-a-waiter. When their eyes met, the man quickly looked away.

"Yeah, something tells me he wants us to see him," Jason said. "But why?"

Scarlet tapped absently on her tablet, then said, "Wait a minute. Duh Megan!" Everyone exchanged a look full of raised eyebrows until she continued, "That mystery boat, the tossed office, now this guy being just shady enough to keep us focused on him." She stared at the others, then added when no one spoke up, "he's a—"

"Distraction," Jason interrupted.

Scarlet tutted, "Well you kinda stole the thunder there, Boss, but yeah." She picked up her tablet, swiping and tapping, then held it up for everyone to see. On the screen was a view from one of the cameras mounted on the exterior of the *Raven*. The mooring next to the *Raven*, the one that had the unnamed boat attached to it when they arrived, was empty.

"Damn," Jason said, standing.

The fake waiter noticed immediately and began walking toward the kitchen door behind the bar.

"Sofia," Jason said.

The ex-marine stood and made a quick line to the front door of the pub.

Jason headed toward the same door the mystery man had just exited through.

"What do we do?" Asako asked Niles.

The large South African put his hand on his friend's. "We do nothing, my friend. When it's time to fight, or shoot, or stab, Jason and Sofia take care of it."

"They're superb at it," Scarlet offered. She looked at the tablet again, then tapped the commset in her ear. "Oracle, go through the camera recordings of the boat that was next to the *Raven* and compile a precis."

"Of course, Scarlet," the AI replied.

"Oh, Oracle, I also uploaded a ton of data from Ms. Yamamoto's server. A precis on that would be excellent."

"Of course."

"Oh, and partition it in a separate secure file folder, please."

"Done."

WHEN JASON ENTERED THE KITCHEN, THERE WAS NO SIGN of the mystery waiter. The cook staff was busy going about their business, only glancing up to see who had intruded into their domain. Jason spotted a door opposite the kitchen from him and rushed toward it.

As the kitchen exit door swung shut behind him, automatically closing, Jason spied the mystery waiter. He was pressed up against the wall of the campus bar by Sofia. The smaller man was wiggling under the much stronger woman's grip.

"Let me go, you crazy bitch!" the younger man spat.

Sofia made a tsking noise. "Do you speak to your abuela like that? No?" She gave the man a shake.

Jason walked up. "Who are you? Why were you keeping us distracted? Did you trash the professor's office?"

The man stared at Jason, then spluttered, "What? Whose office? I don't know what you're talking about. Some guy paid me a hundred bucks to stand around and keep an eye on your group."

"What guy? When was this? How'd he know us?" Jason pressed.

"I don't know man, some dude, never seen him before. He approached me in the quad, like an hour ago."

Sofia looked at Jason. He nodded. "And?"

The not-a-waiter spluttered, "That's it. He pointed you out through the window, gave me the money and walked off." He reached into his pocket and withdrew a crumpled bill. "See!" He tossed it to Jason.

Jason caught the bill, smoothed it out and examined it. He folded it in half and nodded to Sofia. She released her grip on the man. Jason offered him the folded bill. "Get out of here." The kid took off running.

Sofia looked at Jason. "So, what now? Whoever trashed the prof's office was here, saw us. He's good. Hacked the servers here, looking for whatever it is or was he's looking for. Now he's apparently looking for Asako's secret Japanese base."

Jason sighed. "And has a head start." He turned. "Okay, let's get the others and get back to the boat."

PART 2

FIVE

THE RACE IS ON

The walk back to the *Raven* was slower than the walk into campus, thanks to everyone having a box of supplies to carry. Other than the slowness of the walk, nothing eventful happened along the way.

As the group approached the short bridge to the entry hatch of the *Raven*, Jason turned to Sofia. "Sof, you mind stowing all this? I'm gonna get us underway, then we can sit down and talk things out." He knelt down and released one of the mooring lines. Once it went slack, it automatically retracted into the boat.

The muscular Hispanic woman grunted and headed up the boarding ramp, then turned left, heading deeper into the *Raven* toward the cargo hold. Over her shoulder she shouted, "Just leave your boxes inside."

Niles, Asako, and Scarlet went up the ramp, dropping their boxes and heading right at the hatch, making their way toward the bridge.

Jason untied the last mooring line and started up the ramp. He tapped his commset. "Oracle, get the engines started please."

"Acknowledged, Captain," the AI replied politely.

With Oracle's help, it took only a few minutes to navigate the *Raven* out of the slip they had parked in and get back out to sea. Once the boat was heading north at a leisurely clip, Jason had the AI take over and summoned everyone to the lounge area.

Once everyone settled in, Jason looked around. "Okay, so we know someone else is looking for Asako's mysterious Japanese base. We don't know who they are, or precisely what they know." He looked over to Asako, then Scarlet. "Anything specific to add?"

Scarlet rolled forward slightly. "Yeah, quite a lot, actually. I had Oracle prepare a precis for Asako's data and what our dock neighbors were up to when they left. I'll cover Asako's data first, then we can dig into the mystery men." She tapped her tablet, and the big screen TV on the wall clicked, turning on. "First off, Oracle concurs with Asako's interpretation of the data." She nodded toward the small Japanese woman who nodded back, smiling. "Second, while the exact coordinates aren't referenced anywhere in the data, Asako and Oracle again concur, the base is likely somewhere on Graham Island."

Asako raised her hand. "I'd like to add that while the exact location isn't called out, I have several thoughts on that particular subject that, luckily for us, are all in here." She held up a small brown leather notebook, held closed with a strip of leather the same color. "Because the location was never mentioned specifically, I began keeping notes as I pondered the data. Particularly logs and notes written by ship captains and cargo pilots in the margins of manifests and the like." She set the small book down, and after unwinding the leather strap, opened it to show page after page of notes, scribbles, things crossed out.

She nodded to Scarlet, who updated the TV to show Graham Island. "Sadly, no one left a note with *turn right at this feature, then left, then straight on,* but there were enough seemingly random notes to lead me to think the base is somewhere in the Masset Inlet."

Scarlet tapped her tablet screen a few times, and the map on the large TV updated, showing the northernmost section of the island. "I had been wondering how no one had ever discovered a Japanese base, but now it makes sense. Graham is hardly inhabited. The southern section is a nature preserve, and the northern section has only a handful of small fishing villages. Port Clements is the second largest village on the island and has a whopping population of 300 people. Masset, at the opening of the inlet, is the largest with about a thousand people living there. Most of the island is wilderness. Perfect place for a secret military base."

Sofia, who up until then had been sitting quietly in the chair closer to the large TV, studying the maps being displayed, finally said, "So, we have a slightly better idea of exactly where on the island to find the base than our mysterious bad guys, but that's really our only advantage?" She turned to look at the others. "Fun."

Scarlet again tapped her tablet, updating the big screen on the wall. "Actually, the mystery baddies are slightly less mysterious, which I guess brings us to the second precis Oracle created." She pointed to the large screen, showing nearly a dozen men and women, all in black, all carefully keeping their faces hidden from the cameras on the *Raven* as they walked past. "We got bupkis from the cameras, but I got quite a bit from the school's servers."

Jason leaned forward. "You know who they are?"

Scarlet shook her head. "Like names and social security numbers, no. But the virus that was lurking in the chemical and bioengineering department server had some very clear markers, namely the destination for the data that it skimmed." She swiped on her tablet, and the large TV showed a map of Europe. "The data that was skimmed went somewhere in France." The map zoomed in. "Somewhere in or near the campus of Biotech d'Argent, one of the leading biotech and pharmaceutical companies in Europe."

Sofia scratched her chin. "Why would a French biotech company care about a World War Two Japanese base? Even a secret, as-yet-undiscovered one?"

Scarlet leaned back slightly in her chair. "Remember, the virus was spying on the chem and bio department, which makes sense. Anything that department was up to could be interesting to a shifty mega-corporation looking for a leg up on the next big discovery. I bet they've hacked servers all over the world." Her brow wrinkled as she crossed her arms. "If I had to guess, someone in Biotech d'Argent sold or gave this bit of data to someone else to run down."

Jason nodded slowly. "Makes sense. Someone okay with spying on universities to steal tech and ideas would likely have friends in other shady areas of interest." He sighed. "Doesn't help us figure exactly who, but at least gives us some ideas on the type of people we're dealing with. Add in our little adventure in the Pit Pub, and we can be pretty sure they're players, not some amateur adventurers."

Sofia grinned. "Like I said, fun."

MYSTERIOUS MYSTERY

"Okay, well nothing we can do about it now. Everyone might as well hit the sack. It's about seven hundred miles to the northern tip of Graham Island. The *Raven* isn't built for speed; it's gonna be about thirty something hours to get there, so we've got time to work on plans." Jason stood and walked over to the large display screen, turning it off. He looked at the group. "Nothing changes."

Everyone nodded and headed off in various directions. Niles and Asako headed toward the berths, while Scarlet rolled toward the elevator.

Sofia walked over to the refrigerator and withdrew two bottles of beer. She held one up toward Jason, who nodded and came to join her at the kitchen table. "So, pros. European pros, most likely."

"Yeah, this got interesting, didn't it?" He offered his bottle up in a toast. Sofia clinked hers against his. "Tomorrow I'll do some digging and see who might know anything. I can't imagine this would be something Antonio would get into, plus he knows the *Raven*. I don't think he'd be so sneaky as hiring someone to keep us busy."

"Perhaps Eduardo? He's a shithead of the highest order and last I heard, he was skulking about in Portugal," Sofia offered.

Jason shrugged. "Could be Eduardo. He definitely likes to play games." He rubbed his forehead. "I suppose really it could be damn near anyone. I mean, there's no reason that our mystery baddy at Biotech d'Argent wouldn't have American and European shitheads in their Rolodex."

Sofia grunted, then took a long pull of her drink. When she sat the now half empty bottle down, she said, "This is true, and depressing. If we're going that far down *what if road*, it could just be any random merc group. The shady biotech executive could be looking to make a whole new fortune, because let's be honest, he's already rich—"

"He?" Jason smirked.

"Definitely a man." She raised an eyebrow. "Anyway, so Richie Rich wants another fortune. He finds himself some hired guns, maybe an archeologist if he can, and sets out to get richer."

"Believable for sure," Jason agreed.

Sofia emptied her bottle. "Which leaves us where?"

"Same place as before, nowhere good," Jason sighed.

Sofia stood up. "Then off to bed I go. Who knows? Maybe a brilliant idea will reveal itself in my dreams."

"Weirder things have happened," Jason smiled, raising his still half full bottle as she walked through the hatch. He looked at the ceiling. "Oracle, what else can you tell me about Asako's mystery base?"

"Her data is quite extensive and her analysis is, I have to say, impressive. The University wastes her talents in the Asian studies department. She would make a highly competent analyst for any of the security services of the world."

"I'll make sure to tell her. What else?"

"No need. I already did, three minutes ago," the ceiling replied, then continued. "I took the liberty of accessing Japanese public records to correlate some of her findings and found nothing amiss. There almost certainly was a Japanese submarine base on Graham Island. The records she linked, however, do not suggest the base's likely purpose, and I was unable to form my own hypothesis. The Japanese government did an admirable job of keeping the base's purpose, location, and role as vague as possible. Particularly given that they had little to no computing power to help keep the records sorted."

"Is that admiration I hear?" Jason was smiling. He took a sip of his beer.

"It is."

Jason stood up. "Okay. Thanks, Oracle. Keep working on it, and holler if anything comes up." He started toward the hatch leading to the berths.

"Of course, Captain. We're on course and I'll alert you should anything arise. Sleep well."

BREAKFAST

"Good morning, campers!" Jason shouted as Niles and Scarlet entered the lounge.

"Mornin,' Boss!" Scarlet rolled over to the coffeemaker, taking two mugs from the low cupboard. "I got you, Niles. Sit."

"Thank you, my dear," the big African man said, taking a seat. He looked to Jason. "So Jason, I assume you were up most of the night ruminating?" He quirked a lopsided smile.

"Ruminating—you make it sound so scholarly." He turned from the sizzling skillet to look at his friend. "But yeah, I was. Sadly, it didn't accomplish much," he shrugged, "beyond making me tired this morning."

"Pouting never does," Sofia said as she followed Asako into the crew lounge.

Scarlet rolled out of the way to let the two newcomers get at the coffee. "Well, at this point it doesn't much matter, right?" She shrugged. "I mean, we're still heading for the island and last I checked, and I just checked, Oracle hasn't spotted the other ship on radar or on her forward cameras. They're either much faster than we are, or hugging the coast, or went further out to sea."

"And?" Sofia asked, sitting down next to Niles. Asako piled in next to her.

"And, none of that is material to right now." She pointed to the table for emphasis. "Right now, we need to get to the island, have a plan, then deal with whatever comes." She leaned back and took a sip of her coffee.

"Very bold, chica." Sofia nodded in approval, then looked around the room. "She's not wrong. There's nothing to do right now but plan and try to be ready for whatever we encounter." She thunked her mug on the table twice. "But first, where's breakfast?"

Jason turned around with the skillet in one hand and a long spatula in the other. "Right here. Scrambled eggs with peppers and a little secret sauce."

"Secret sauce?" Asako said, offering her plate as Jason slipped a heap of eggs on to it.

Sofia gave the petite Asian woman a gentle nudge. "He's full of shit. The secret sauce is hot sauce, some brand he won't share that he picks up in Hong Kong whenever he goes. Keeps it locked in his berth." She rolled her eyes.

Jason left and returned with a plate of bacon. "Exactly, secret." He sat down and scooped a fork full of eggs into his mouth. Around the eggs he said, "So good."

"That is some secret. Surely a group such as this has ferreted out the secret? There can't be that many hot sauce shops in Hong Kong?"

Scarlet laughed. "Oh, we've tried." She pointed at Sofia. "She tried trailing him for a full day. Nothing." Her finger moved to Niles. "He tried jimmying the lock on Jason's room back at base. Nothing."

Asako looked at Scarlet, her eyes narrowing. "And you?"

Scarlet looked up at the ceiling and whistled.

Jason looked at the team hacker. "What did you do?"

Scarlet turned to Jason, a Cheshire Cat grin on her face. "Your secret is safe with me, Boss man."

Niles released a booming laugh, turning to Sofia. "We should have known."

Breakfast proceeded with small talk until every plate was empty and the bacon plate was barren. Jason got up to clear the dishes and Scarlet rolled over to the big screen, pulling her tablet out of its pouch on the side of her chair. "Asako, I'd love your input on some things. Oracle and I spent some time last night trying to work out some likely locations for your base."

"Of course," Asako said, sliding out of her seat and walking over to join Scarlet by the TV.

Jason closed the dishwasher and turned to Sofia. "Mind helping me in the engine room?"

"Seguro." The two headed out the hatch and aft toward the stairs to the lower decks.

Niles looked around and leaned back in his seat, watching his friend and Scarlet work, taking a sip of his coffee.

BEST DINNER EVER

THE DAY PASSED QUIETLY; JASON AND SOFIA SPENT MOST OF it in the engine room tinkering. One of the two powerful MTU Diesel engines had been acting up during the last outing, so Jason wanted to make sure it was in tip top shape for what was to come. Scarlet worked with Asako for several hours, then retired to the Ops Center to work on her own projects. Niles and Asako ate lunch and sat on the bow lounge area, enjoying the view as Vancouver Island slid past them. They passed only a handful of boats, all pleasure craft of varying sizes, none passing less than a mile or so distant.

By the time everyone sat down for dinner, Jason and Sofia were tired and covered in grease.

"Seriously, you couldn't have taken a shower before dinner?" Scarlet said as Jason slid into the seat next to where she was parked. "Oh, sweet boneless Christ, you stink!" She pushed against him.

Jason blew her a kiss. "Sorry, we lost track of time and I didn't want to delay the meal." He looked over to Niles slaving away at the cooktop. "Plus, I didn't want to take a chance I'd miss out on this." His grin was both genuine and as wide as his face.

"I admit I'm intrigued," Asako said from her spot at the table, next to Sofia. "Niles ushered me away some time ago, and wouldn't let me help him or even be in here until a few minutes ago. What is so exciting?"

Niles turned around with a large platter loaded with fried something or other.

"Vetkoek!" Scarlet clapped her hands, urging the big South African anthropologist closer. She took the platter, taking two of the fried balls, and passed the plate to Jason.

When Niles turned again with a large cast-iron pot, Scarlet pumped her fist in the air. "Bredie! Oh man, Niles, you spoil us!" The large man grinned.

Asako watched the entire exchange before saying, "Niles, I had no idea you cooked. Is this traditional South African fare?"

"It is indeed, my dear," he said as he took a seat at the table. Everyone had taken a fried morsel or two and had a bowl full of the hearty stew.

Asako took a bite of her vetkoek and moaned, then upon seeing everyone look at her, blushed. "Niles..."

"Right?" Scarlet agreed. "Now you see why Captain B.O. didn't want to risk it." She glanced at Jason. "Even if he should have." She pinched her nose and ate a spoonful of stew.

"Excuse the interruption, but a vessel is on an intercept course with us," Oracle said from the overhead speaker. "It is currently ten miles off."

Jason looked up. "Can you identify the vessel? Name, registration?"

"Unfortunately, no. It lacks both and is not transmitting any identification," the AI replied.

Sofia looked at Jason, the ceiling. "Could it be the same boat from the University dock?"

"Processing." Everyone was eating as fast as they could. "The probability that this vessel is the same as the one we observed at the University dock is forty-two percent, so unlikely," Oracle finally said.

Without another word, everyone slid out of their seats and put their plates and bowls in the sink.

Asako watched, and as Jason and Sofia hurried out of the room, she turned to Niles. "What is happening?"

The big black man shrugged. "It would appear that someone is en route to pay us a visit." He looked at the large TV. "Oracle, please display our current location and the path the unidentified vessel took on its approach."

The screen lit up, showing an overhead map view. The *Raven* was just past the northernmost tip of Vancouver Island. The red oval representing the unidentified boat had a dotted line from it to somewhere on the eastern side of the island. He nodded. "As I expected. A trap."

"What do we do?" the worried Asian woman said, her hand grasping Niles' arm.

"We go to the Ops Center and help however we can. Fret not, the *Raven* is not defenseless, and her captain is quite skilled as a sailor." He smiled as he guided her out of the lounge and toward the stairwell leading down.

SIX

PARTY CRASHERS

"Interesting. Not our friends from the University, that's for sure," Jason said as he studied one of the displays on the bridge.

Sofia was looking at the same monitor, then looked up out the bridge window. "Run-of-the-mill pirates?"

"That's my guess. Just crappy timing," Jason replied. He tapped a control. "You all set up down there?"

"Yup, all set, Jason. I've got Niles and Asako set up and ready." There was a pause, and Scarlet lowered her voice. "Pirates?"

"Probably." He killed the connection and looked at Sofia. "Let's go get dressed for the party."

The presumed pirates were in an old fishing boat that they had converted to their purposes. They had mounted a jury-rigged heavy machine gun on the bow, and several sheets of corrugated steel were bolted to the small superstructure around the pilot's box.

As the other boat pulled alongside the *Raven*, several powerful searchlights ignited, bathing the *Raven* in light. Jason and Sofia crab-walked out of the flying bridge to the railing. Jason nodded, and Sofia popped up and fired a short burst into one of the lights. As she dropped, Jason stood and took out another search light. It took him three shots with his pistol. From the other boat, several people began shouting. Sofia stood and took aim at a man trying to swing the heavy machine gun around, dropping him with two shots to the chest. Jason looked over to Sofia, nodded, and both of them jumped over the railing onto the deck of the pirate ship.

On the deck of the other boat, Sofia looked over. "Three shots?"

"I've been busy. I'll practice more," Jason replied.

Two pirates burst from a hatch, one with a rifle, the other a shotgun. "Freeze!" The one with the shotgun shouted in heavily accented English.

Jason and Sofia raised their arms, letting their rifle and pistol fall to the deck. "What the fuck? You're not supposed to board us!" the one with the rifle shouted.

The other nodded vigorously, adding, "You wait for us to board you and give us all your shit!"

Jason shrugged. "Sorry. Happy to go back over there and wait."

From over the sound of the ocean, a faint whirring sound built. Shotgun and Rifle both looked at each other, then at their prisoners. Rifle waved his weapon. "Come on, inside. We have to secure your ship."

The whirring grew louder. "What is that?" Shotgun asked Rifle, looking around frantically.

Jason smiled as Shotgun fell to the deck, a small dart stuck in his neck.

"The fu—" Rifle said, then also collapsed.

"Go kick pirate booty, Boss!" Scarlet said over the commsets, then added, "Ha, booty."

Jason and Sofia grabbed their weapons, Sofia stowing her rifle on her back, opting for her own pistol, drawing it from the holster on her hip. She looked at her boss and nodded.

They rushed through the hatch the two now unconscious pirates had just come through.

"So, uh, what do we do now?" Asako asked from the workstation she was sitting at in the Ops Center. She was staring at the screen showing the pirate vessel resting against the *Raven*.

Niles rested his hand on hers. "Nothing. We're just here in case the wizard over there needs anything."

Scarlet, her back to the two of them, raised her hand. "That'd be me." She looked over her shoulder, grinning. "Actually, I could use a ZapPow."

Asako looked at Niles, her confusion obvious. The African man stood and went to a small cooler, retrieving a can of something. He held the drink up so that Asako could see it. On the can the word *ZapPow* was written in bright green block letters with lightning bolts shooting out in all directions. He deposited the beverage in Scarlet's open hand.

After a loud sip of the super-caffeinated beverage, Scarlet extended both arms in front of her, palms out, cracking her knuckles. "Okay, time to introduce some pirates to my friends, Edward and Jacob." She tapped a few comments into one of the computers within arm's reach, and two large displays came to life. The screens started dark but shifted to the green of night vision cameras. The view on each display tilted as the drones quickly rose above the *Raven*.

Scarlet looked over at her two guests. "I'm partial to team Jacob, but Edward has slightly better targeting sensors."

Asako looked at Niles, who shrugged.

On the two displays, the pirate vessel came into view. Two pirates had weapons trained on Sofia and Jason. Scarlet grunted, "Well, that didn't take long." She reached over and tapped a keyboard under one monitor. Both screens flashed, and small red rectangles appeared, moving slowing around the screen. On the left screen, the rectangle settled on one of the pirates. "See, Edward's just a bit faster on the draw." Asako now realized that the drone on the screen was named Edward. On the other screen, the red rectangle had settled and the pirate it had settled on was falling to the deck.

"Go kick pirate booty, Boss!" Scarlet said, then added, "Ha, booty." She turned to Asako and Niles, putting her hand over the mic on her headset. "That was good, right?"

NOT ALL PIRATES

THE PIRATE SHIP WAS ONLY ABOUT HALF AS BIG AS THE
Raven but somehow had more corridors than Jason had ever
seen on a ship that size. He was about to comment on this to
Sofia, when a hatch swung open, right into him. Sofia was three
steps ahead of him. "Ouch!" Before he could get around the
hatch, two gunshots rang out. Pushing the hatch closed he
groused, "Who has hatches that open out into the corridor?
That's not safe!" He swung it open and looked down at the two
dead pirates. "Shame on you."

Sofia tsked. "Come on, there can't be many more, and they
don't seem to even know we're aboard."

As if in answer, the overhead speaker nearest them came to
life. "Phillip and Marcel are down! They have boarded us!"

"Uh, Boss, two more are on deck now," Scarlet reported
from the *Raven*. "I think they're coming over. Yup, they are
indeed boarding us."

Jason looked at Sofia and they both headed further into the
pirate ship, a staircase ahead likely leading to the bridge up
above. Jason tapped his commset. "Scar, you know what to do."

"Roger that," the hacker replied.

Sofia reached the stairs first and began climbing, with Jason a few steps behind her.

SCARLET TURNED TO THE ACADEMICS SEATED AT THE SMALL table in the corner of the Ops Center. "We've got two uninvited guests." She turned back to her screens.

Niles looked at the screens, then at Asako. "We've been through this before. Don't worry." He pointed to one of the screens, a camera mounted outside the *Raven* somewhere, looking at the forward deck area. Two pirates were creeping around the bow of the ship, heading for the open lounge area.

"Operation ghost boat starts, now," Scarlet said to no one in particular. On the screen, the pirates had entered the main crew lounge. The sliding glass door they'd entered through stood wide open until it slammed shut. Powerful magnetic locks engaged. The two pirates spun, and one frantically fired a short burst from his submachine gun. The thick, bullet-proof glass didn't even scuff from the impacts.

"Bullet-proof glass?" Asako wondered aloud. "Neat."

Niles nodded. "As I said, not our first time with pirates and other assorted bad guys."

On the screen, the two pirates split up, one heading for the stairs to the bridge above, the other to the hatch and the stairs leading down a level.

Scarlet turned again. "Think they'll enjoy Rufus?" Her grin was feral.

Niles tutted, "I know *you* will." He shuddered.

Scarlet shrugged, turning back to her monitors. "True." She tapped a control and the hatch to the bridge slammed shut, nearly taking off the head of the pirate on the stairs. The startled man fell back to the deck. He stood, looking around, never spotting the camera. He was about to head for the hatch his companion had taken when that hatch slammed shut in front of him. He looked around, his gun tracking back and forth.

"Scarlet, the other pirate is in Niles' quarters now," Oracle announced from the ceiling speaker.

"My quarters? Why that miserable—" Niles began, only to be cut off by Scarlet.

"Don't worry, professor, he's about to meet Rufus. Touching your stuff will be the last thing on his mind."

SOFIA POKED HER HEAD UP INTO THE BRIDGE JUST ENOUGH to see three people huddled over the boat's controls; one spoke frantically into a handheld radio, in French. She looked down at Jason, held up three fingers, then pulled a small canister from her utility belt. She tossed the small device into the middle of the group of men, and as they looked down in surprise, the device exploded with a bright flash. Sofia pulled herself up the final stairs into the room, lunging for the nearest pirate.

Jason came up a second later, tackling another of the men. The man he'd tackled turned out to have hand-to-hand combat training and deftly blocked Jason's follow up punch, landing his own in Jason's midsection. As Jason fell backward, a laptop sailed over his head to smash into the face of his opponent. The pirate crumpled to the ground, holding his nose and groaning. Jason looked over in time to see Sofia expertly fending off both pirates.

Standing, he cleared his throat. "Excuse me." The three combatants stopped and turned to him. He pointed to the pirates. "She just took this dude out." He turned to the pirate on the ground, who happened to be trying to get up, and leaned down, punching the man in the face, causing the bloodied pirate to collapse unconscious. "By throwing a laptop at him, while still holding you two off. Might be this is the time to cut your losses."

YOU SCREAM, I SCREAM

THE PIRATE WANDERING AROUND THE CREW QUARTERS level was pulling open drawer after drawer in Niles' quarters when something in the corridor thunked, then thunked again. The pirate looked at the open door. "Georgie?" he shouted. Nothing.

The pirate looked one last time in the drawer he had open, then closed it, turning to exit the room. Something shot past the open hatch, much too fast for him to see in the low light. He snapped his rifle up. "Georgie, what are you doing?" he demanded. Nothing.

He poked his head out into the corridor, looking up and down the length of it. Nothing, no sign of his friend. The hatch at the top of the stairs was still closed. The pirate shrugged and headed for the hatch across from Niles' quarters. As he touched the lever handle, something down at the aft end of the corridor made a low gurgling noise. A green glow shone from under the furthest door.

"What the fuck is happening here?" the pirate asked aloud. He turned back to the stairwell and hatch leading back up to the crew lounge. Closed. "Cái quái g"vậy?"

From the opposite end of the corridor, another thunk echoed. The pirate turned back to look down the length of the corridor, hatches on either side leading to each member of the crew's quarters, all closed. He moved back toward the room across from Niles' when the locking mechanism on the hatch engaged, *thudding* into place. Then the next door followed, and the next, each lock slamming home with a loud clack, one at a time. The pirate crossed himself. "Hello? I just want to go home now. I did not mean to intrude." He nervously looked left and right as he began to walk toward the far end of the corridor, the hatch leading to the stairs down to the next deck, and the elevator that spanned all the decks of the *Raven*.

The last hatch before the watertight hatch, and the stairs down, was still glowing green. It was the only open hatch in the corridor. What looked like smoke began billowing over the threshold, filling the corridor. The pirate stopped dead in his tracks only five feet from the open hatch and its green glow.

A loud *thunk* came from an open hatch, followed by another. A long leg that looked like it was made of an unholy combination of metal and flesh crossed the threshold.

"Ôi chúa ơi!" the pirate screamed as he dropped to his knees.

The thing attached to the leg cleared the threshold of the hatch; smoke swirled about its feet. It was only about five feet tall, a maze of wires and metal framework with what looked like flesh stretched across sections of it. A head that was half human and half machine turned to peer at the kneeling pirate, while a blue eye and a glowing red lens focused on the terrified man. When it opened its mouth, nothing came out but a scream that caused the pirate to flinch and lose control of his bladder.

"Oh man! I think he peed!" Scarlet said as she, Niles, and Asako watched on one of the large displays in the Ops Center.

On the screen, the half machine, half human creature lumbered toward the pirate still frozen with fear and kneeling on the floor. The machine rocked back and forth as it walked, its jerky motion making it look drunk.

"I need to work on his gyroscopic guidance. He still looks like he's a step away from falling over," Scarlet observed.

From the speaker in her headset, Jason's voice said, "We've got the last of the pirates tied up. How's things over there?"

Scarlet tapped her headset. "We've got one locked up in the lounge, and the other is in crew quarters meeting Rufus."

"If he pees on the deck, you have to clean it," Jason replied.

"We have a Roomba, it's fine," Scarlet retorted, then looked at Niles and mouthed the words, *How did he know?* Niles shrugged.

On the screen, Rufus was barely a foot from the still cowering pirate.

Scarlet cackled and pushed a button on one of her keyboards. On the screen, Rufus opened his mouth, but instead of the horrific scream, a stream of sticky green goop shot out, covering the pirate. The man flinched and fell on his back thrashing wildly, screaming.

On a nearby monitor, Jason and Sofia had climbed the boarding ladder from the pirate's ship and were standing outside the rounded glass wall of the lounge. After a minute, the man dropped his submachine gun and knelt on the carpeted deck, fingers interlaced behind his head.

Jason looked at one of the cameras. "If you're done playing, we've got the other one." On the display, he was smiling at the camera.

"Yup, he's all yours," Scarlet replied. She pressed a few keys and the corridor lighting returned to normal. Small vents sucked the smoke out as the green light in the storage room turned off. Rufus turned and shambled back to his storage area. The object that had shot past the door earlier slid back along the track in the ceiling toward a small storage box near Rufus' storage closet. The terrified pirate raised his head from his arms and looked around in time to see that the object was a basketball painted black. He jumped when the hatch to the crew lounge opened and Sofia descended, her pistol at the ready.

Asako looked at Niles. "You people are demented."

BACK ON TRACK

"ARE YOU SURE IT'S SAFE TO JUST LEAVE THEM?" ASAKO
asked as the *Raven* pulled away from the pirate vessel. Everyone
was together on the bridge watching the other boat recede on a
monitor.

Jason nodded. "Yeah. For one thing, Sofia and I made sure
it's not going anywhere anytime soon. And two, we called it in
to the Canadian authorities, so someone should be along eventu-
ally to pick them up."

Scarlet, smiling, added, "Plus, I uploaded a little virus into
their computer. Might I add, their gear was horribly ancient. I
don't know who they typically prey on, but sheesh." She waved
a hand dismissively. "Anyhow, I wiped most of the navigation
data from the calculator that ran things over there. Even if their
engines worked, they'd have no clue where to go or how to get
there."

Niles offered Sofia a beer, then moved over to Jason, offering
the same. "I noticed that our boarders were Asian, Vietnamese?"

Asako nodded. "Got it in one, my friend." She smiled, then
continued, "You have a good ear for language. I wonder what

Vietnamese pirates would be doing on this side of the Pacific? Certainly, that boat of theirs couldn't have made the crossing?"

Jason engaged the autopilot and spun his chair around. "With the sea level rise and Chinese expansion, there's a diaspora happening. I'm sure the Chinese aren't talking about it. The US certainly isn't." He headed for the hatch and the stairs down into the boat. "I'm heading to bed. See you all in the morning." Everyone nodded as he vanished through the open hatch.

Scarlet's eyes narrowed, and she cast a glance at Sofia, then Niles. "Bomberman?"

"Oh, hell yeah," Sofia said, pushing herself out of the co-pilot's chair she was lounging in.

Asako looked at Niles, an eyebrow arched. He grinned and took her hand. "Come!"

THE LARGE DISPLAY IN THE *RAVEN'S* MAIN LOUNGE WAS not only excellent for presentations, but also a great display for video games. On the eighty-inch display, four small helmeted characters were running around a two-dimensional map, trying their best to blow each other up with assorted bombs.

One of the characters, a pink one, got too close to a bomb and was caught in the blast. "Damnit!" Asako growled.

Scarlet looked over. "Too slow!" As she looked back at the screen, her own little bomb-throwing spaceman exploded, caught in the blast of a four-way bomb. "Sonofabitch!"

Niles tutted, "You were saying something about being too slow?"

"Eyes on the prize, old man," Sofia said, not taking her own eyes off the massive screen on the wall. Her character was moving toward Niles' in the opposite corner of the game board.

"Oh no you don't, young lady!" the heavyset South African man chortled, working his controller.

Asako looked at Scarlet. "I don't know how you all can drink beers and play video games, or sleep in Jason's case, so soon after nearly being killed by pirates."

Scarlet smiled at the Asian woman. "Oh prof, you've no idea. Those bozos? Not really a threat. We've faced way worse." She turned back to the screen. "Watch out, Niles!"

Too late, Sofia's small bomb-throwing spaceman had succeeded in surrounding Niles' with cartoonish bombs fencing him in.

"Fok!"

"Less gloating, more bombing," Sofia said, turning around to look at the others. "With that, I am going to bed." She stood and put her empty beer bottle in the recycling bin. "Buenas noches."

In his quarters, Jason was sitting at the small desk built into the corner of the room. The laptop on the desk showed their current position heading just past halfway to Graham Island. "What secrets are you hiding?" he asked the display.

"I'm sorry, were you speaking to me, Captain?" Oracle asked.

Jason put a hand to his eyes, then looked up. "No, Oracle, sorry. Was asking a rhetorical question out loud. Privacy mode, please."

"I see. Privacy mode engaged." A soft tone sounded, letting Jason know that Oracle was no longer actively monitoring his quarters.

He turned back to the laptop, moving the cursor a bit to

show the Masset Inlet. He absently tapped the display as he stared at the screen. "Who else is looking for you?"

SEVEN

THOSE AREN'T GOOD OPTIONS

"Good morning, everyone," Asako said as she entered the *Raven's* lounge. The smell of coffee and bacon had brought everyone to the space. Niles raised his mug in greeting as Scarlet rolled over, balancing two mugs precariously on the arm of her chair. She offered one to Asako, who took it, bowing. Scarlet giggled.

Jason turned from the stove. "We'll be in range of Graham Island by lunchtime." He moved to the table and deposited the eggs he'd been preparing on the plate in the middle of the table. Turning back to the stove, he added, "Still a day or so to get around to the top of the island where the inlet is."

Asako looked out the nearest window facing north. "How dangerous do you think it will be?"

Jason shrugged. "Well, we still don't know who that other boat belonged to, but we know they're at least semi-related to what we're doing, so—"

Scarlet interrupted, "Which always means they're bad guys."

Jason turned, eyebrow quirked. "So, yeah, the odds are good they don't want us to beat them to the punch, even if none of us knows what that is, exactly." He gestured toward Asako with a long fork. "Thanks to you, we have a few small advantages, though. Namely a starting point, the Masset Inlet."

Sofia scooped some eggs on her plate, then said, "Last time I looked at the map of the island, that's still a lot of ground to cover."

Jason nodded. "It is, but I've been noodling on that for a bit and have some thoughts." He threw a few more pieces of bacon on the skillet. Over the sizzling, he added, "I'll go over those with Asako after breakfast, but in the meantime, we still have the mysterious boat folks to think about. In theory, we were right on their tail, but then our Vietnamese friends delayed us an hour or so. I didn't want to tax the engines, or our fuel reserves, so we've kept a constant speed." He came to the table, plate of bacon in hand. "The other folks likely don't have any clue where to start so are almost certainly waiting for us, somewhere in the island's vicinity."

"Cheery," Niles said, grabbing two strips of bacon. He dropped them on his plate, blowing on his fingers.

Scarlet looked up from her tablet and took a bite of eggs, followed by bacon. In between chews, she said, "Okay... so I think... If we take the... west side of the..."

"Stop," Jason said before she continued. "Chew, then talk." He put a hand in front of his eyes.

The young hacker nodded, chewed, and swallowed. "Okay, like I was saying. If we take the western side of the island, we might be able to sneak into the inlet without them seeing." She tapped the tablet, and the main display across the room turned on. The huge screen displayed the northern half of Graham Island. "It's riskier. We'll be in open water, but it's pretty safe to assume the baddies will assume we'd take the safer passage between the island and the mainland." To show her point, a bright pink, hand-drawn squiggle moved from their current position up between the island and the mainland, toward the opening of the inlet. Another equally hand-drawn line, this one red, started at the same point but went out around the western edge of the island. "We don't lose much time, especially if we adjust course now," she added, then took another frighteningly big bite of her breakfast. Everyone watched her chew.

Jason stared at the screen, then looked at the ceiling. "Oracle, what do you think of taking the open water approach?"

From the speaker nearest the kitchenette table, the ship's AI answered, "Scarlet is correct regarding the overall time involved. Both routes are approximately the same amount of time. I accessed the Canadian weather service, and the only risk I foresee with the open water approach is a storm several miles offshore. It is impossible to determine whether it will arrive while we are in open water or not, given its currently varied speed over the ocean. The weather service has categorized the storm *potentially pre-hurricane*. It could affect us, or not."

"So, fifty-fifty," Niles said to nods from the rest of the table.

Everyone silently stared at each other until Sofia sighed loud enough to make Asako jump. "So we go the open sea route, right? I mean, we can speed up, maybe miss the storm. We can't do anything about the baddies likely waiting for us."

Everyone nodded. Jason slowly chewed a bite of bacon.

SO BUMPY

"WELL, THIS WENT ABOUT HOW WE SHOULD HAVE expected," Jason said. He was in his seat on the bridge, hands gripping the controls tightly. The *Raven* was bouncing around in ten-foot waves.

"I suppose when we agreed it was the easiest route, we should have known better," Sofia offered from her seat next to him. She was doing her best to scan the nearby water for problems their sensors might miss. The rest of the team and their client-slash-guest Asako were in the Ops Center, ostensibly the safest part of the boat. The lounge below the bridge was buttoned up against the waves that were routinely washing over the deck of the converted luxury yacht.

Jason nodded, "Yeah, you'd think at least one of us would know better by now." He glanced at the radar display between his seat and Sofia's. The thunderstorm that three hours ago had been fifty miles out had picked up speed and intensity quicker than the Canadian weather service had expected. The *Raven* crested a particularly large wave and plunged into the trough, causing Jason's stomach, and probably everyone else's onboard, to flip flop. He looked at Sofia. "You think Asako gets seasick?"

"A little late now, don't you think?" She didn't bother to look at him, her eyes glued to the forward window. A few miles off to their right, the shore of Graham Island was barely visible through the driving rain, mostly visible during flashes of lightning.

"I MIGHT BE SICK," ASAKO SAID, HER HEAD IN HER FOLDED arms on the small table in the Ops Center. Niles reached for a small airsickness bag in a pocket attached to the bulkhead and wordlessly offered it to her, tapping it against her hand. Without lifting her head, she clutched the bag.

"Please, no hurling in the Ops Center," Scarlet said from her station, the sections that folded out securing her chair in place.

Niles scooted a little further from his friend. "I can escort you to the head if you'd like."

Asako shook her head, still buried in her arms. "I know the way." As the boat settled between waves, she took the moment of stillness to bolt from the room.

Scarlet watched her go, then turned to Niles. "Guess rough seas aren't something Asian studies professors normally encounter?"

Niles grunted. "They're not something archeologists typically encounter, either." The room, and the surrounding *Raven* surged up a wave, leaving their stomachs several feet below.

Scarlet turned her attention back to the myriad screens around her workstation. "Jason, looks like we're nearing the northern tip." She turned to Niles. "The tip," she said, chuckling. Niles sighed loud enough that Jason and Sofia probably heard it over the comms.

"Roger that, Scar. I see it," Jason replied. Through the up

and down, roller coaster motion, the *Raven* tilted to the starboard, adding a new axis to the twisting and turning.

From outside the Ops Center, Niles and Scarlet heard Asako groan, "Oh God!" followed by the slamming of the hatch to the lavatory just down the corridor.

Niles and Scarlet exchanged a look. Then the young hacker turned back to her consoles. She leaned in toward the display showing the radar return. "This thing turned wicked fast."

Niles nodded slowly, taking a sip from the water bottle in the holder next to him. "Indeed it did. I've heard that the North Pacific storms have been getting more and more intense lately."

"Climate change ain't real, though," Scarlet said in a mocking tone as the *Raven* lurched upward violently and almost as violently crashed back down, her hull groaning.

"There it is," Sofia said, pointing.

"I see it," Jason replied, easing the controls to starboard, guiding the *Raven* closer to the island and the Northern tip, a blunt promontory. "See anything?"

The Hispanic ex-marine stared intently at the radar display. The upside of the *Raven* having previously been owned by a drug cartel boss was that her sensor suite was state of the art—before Jason got it and started making upgrades.

"No, wait. Yup. Mierda, they're parked right at the opening of the inlet." She turned and looked at Jason, who was still gripping the controls tightly as the *Raven* rose and fell through the swells.

WILD GOOSE CHASES

"Think we can slip past?" Jason asked over the rain lashing against the windows. The blackness outside was broken momentarily by a flash of lightning ripping across the sky.

"No chance," Sofia replied.

"Boss man, we're monitoring down here, I think..." Scarlet said, then stopped as the *Raven* plunged into a large trough between swells. "Oh, that was interesting. Anyway, I think I can configure the twins to look like us, maybe lead the baddies far enough away from the opening so we can slip through."

Jason looked at Sofia, who shrugged, then said, "Okay, give it a shot. They can fly in this mess, right?"

"Should be able to. The wind speed isn't that high," the young hacker replied from below decks.

The *Raven* rose and dipped again, tilting severely to port as a swell caught her in her turn toward the island.

"Okay, maybe it's a little windy, but should be okay," Scarlet added.

Jason and Sofia exchanged another look. On a monitor overhead, they watched as the two drones departed from their storage units near the aft of the *Raven*. The lids of the small hangar closed after the drones departed.

On the radar display, two small dots appeared, racing through the storm. While Jason and Sofia watched, the two dots moved and came together, and from one radar sweep to the next, they became a single dot closer in size to the *Raven*.

Sofia glanced over to Jason, her eyebrows raised. "That's impressive. How'd she do that?"

Jason shrugged. "Beats me." He tilted his head, chin guiding Sofia's attention back to the radar display. On it, the dot they assumed was their friends from the University docks was beginning to move, shifting to head toward the fake *Raven*.

"She needs a raise," Sofia murmured.

"Never tell her that," Jason said. "Her head is big enough as it is."

"She's also on comms," Scarlet said from the overhead speaker.

"Shit," Jason grumbled, then added, "you're not getting a raise, but great work."

"Your praise is all the payment I desire," Scarlet said. Over the speaker, it wasn't clear if she was being sincere or not.

Sofia snapped her fingers, bringing Jason's focus back. "They're totally buying it. Time to see how good that radar absorbing paint you bought is."

Jason pushed the throttle forward, driving the *Raven* through a swell, raining water down on the deck with a roar. "For what it cost, it better work," he said, eyes not leaving the view out the forward windows. He reached over and pressed a few buttons on the panel down by his leg. "Just in case."

Throughout the boat, the sound of machinery rose.

"WHAT'S THAT?" ASAKO ASKED AS THE GRINDING NOISE built.

"The weapons. Jason must not think the diversion with the drones will work," Niles offered.

Scarlet shook her fist. "The twins won't let us down." Under her breath she added, "I hope."

Niles shook his head and turned to Asako. "The *Raven* has several hidden automated weapons emplacements. Nothing too big, a few auto cannons fore and aft."

"Machine guns? Hidden machine guns?"

Niles shrugged. "I think there is a difference. I very much remember Sofia lecturing me once."

"No, I mean, if this vessel has automatic machine guns, why were they not used when those pirates attacked us?" the flustered Asian woman asked, a flush creeping up her neck.

"Oh!" Niles nodded. "Yes, well, Jason prefers to not use them unless he has to. They're highly illegal, as you can imagine."

"Ammo ain't cheap, either," Scarlet offered.

"How could I imagine that? I'm a college professor, an Asian studies professor!" the now more-than-a-little irritated Asian woman shouted.

Scarlet didn't turn from her screens, guiding the twin drones further away from the island and the only way into the inlet within the island. "This is why we don't tell people about the *Raven's* extra features."

Asako sighed and slumped in her seat.

The two matte black drones headed further out to sea, their four propellers fighting to keep each drone airborne through the storm.

FIRST OFF THE BLOCK

THE STORM RAGING ACROSS THE NORTHERN HALF OF Graham Island was a bit less severe in the river leading to the Masset Inlet. The nearly mile wide river was much calmer than the seas beyond it.

Jason looked up. "We're in the inlet. Should be a bit smoother." He glanced down at the radar display. The dot representing the twins had turned toward the mainland. "Wonder how long they'll buy that?"

"Why would you ask that?" Sofia asked, turning to look at him, her expression grim. The radar display beeped and drew her attention back. "Dios mio." She jabbed an accusing finger at the display. "See what you did?" The dot that represented the twins had vanished.

Jason looked back at the ceiling. "Hey, Scar, your drones seem to have vanished."

A string of cursing came over the speaker followed by Niles' voice. "Yes, I believe she is aware. Before she started screaming, she mentioned that one of them was having a receiver problem," the thick South African archeologist offered.

The dot representing the other, still unidentified, boat began to turn.

"Shit, they'll be back on us in no time, unless they sink, but I doubt we'll be that lucky," Jason said.

Sofia shook her head. "Good call. Can we go faster?"

Jason shook his head. "No, the computer doesn't have depth data on this channel, so we can only go as fast as the sonar can map it. Running aground here would only help whoever that is."

"I am attempting to map the channel as quickly as possible, Captain," Oracle offered.

Jason smiled. "That wasn't a criticism. It's all good." He looked at the ceiling. "Scar, did we lose both drones?"

"No, Edward, is still on the board. Poor Jacob. Edward's on auto-nav back to the *Raven*, hugging the waves to be harder to detect."

"Okay, send Asako up. We'll be in the inlet in another half hour, then she'll need to show me the way."

"She's on her way," Scarlet replied.

"Okay, cool. Now, about Edward. Can it harass that other boat? I promise if it buys the farm, I'll buy you a new one."

"Uh, you were buying me a new one anyway. Remember Jacob? He's dead."

"*He* is a drone, but okay, sure. I'll get you two drones," Jason sighed, rolling his eyes.

"I heard that."

Sofia turned, suppressing a chuckle.

"Just do it, Scarlet," Jason said.

On the radar display, a dot appeared slightly ahead of their mysterious pursuers. It turned and headed straight for the other boat. Over the speakers, Scarlet's voice softly said, "Godspeed Edward, Godspeed."

"That's not healthy," Sofia said, looking up to see if they had heard her.

On the radar display, the Edward-dot was circling the other dot, the mysterious boat from the University dock. The Edward-dot would circle, then rush toward the other dot, then withdraw. Both drones were equipped with small caliber machine guns, not powerful enough to damage the pursuing craft, but certainly enough to distract the pilot as bullets pinged off the bridge glass. Edward had about one hundred rounds.

As if reading Jason's mind, Scarlet answered the question he was about to ask. "Edward has only about twenty minutes of battery left. Fighting the storm plus that little radar spoofing bit are battery killers. Firing his gun doesn't help, either."

"Well, good work. You bought us a nice head start," Jason offered. He looked at the radar display. The pursuing boat had slowed down enough that it was nearly at the edge of the display.

Asako walked onto the bridge. "Did we lose them?" She looked out the windows.

"Kinda. They know we're here somewhere but hopefully can't see us. We'll be out of the channel in a bit. Time to share your secrets on where you think the base is."

The petite woman nodded. "Of course." She walked over to a map of the island that was being displayed on a monitor near the back of the bridge. To fit the island, the monitor had been rotated ninety degrees so it was now taller than wide. She studied the map for a few minutes. Jason and Sofia exchanged glances. Jason was about to ask if the professor needed help when she finally said, "From what I pieced together, I believe the base is somewhere here in this western portion of the inlet. More or less directly opposite Port Clements." She had a finger resting on the display over the western shore and a small island no more than a mile long sat in the middle of a cove a few miles wide. "Beyond this island."

Jason worked the controls and pushed the throttle forward a bit more. He looked up. "Oracle, we good for more speed?"

"We are, Captain. The bed of the channel has been deepening for the last mile. I believe it is safe to further increase our speed."

He pushed the throttles further forward. "Let's get there, then." He turned to Sofia. "Better get the launch ready."

The Hispanic woman nodded. "Come on, Doc." She tapped the small Asian woman on the shoulder as she departed the bridge.

EIGHT

ALL ASHORE WHO'S GOING ASHORE

It took almost an hour to exit the channel and cross the inlet. Jason kept the *Raven* near the northern side of the inlet on the off chance someone in Port Clements might be looking out into the inlet. Why that might happen in the middle of a storm he couldn't guess, but Canadians did weird things like looking out into storms.

The *Raven* sailed a bit longer until, "I've anchored us on the southwest side of the island. Hopefully that'll keep her out of sight as our friends come in looking for us. We lucked out in that whatever Edward—"

"May he rest in peace," Scarlet interrupted.

Jason groaned. "Yes, anyway. Whatever he did slowed them enough that we made it here before I saw them on radar again. I've shut everything down, so we should be damn near invisible. The storm is helping on that front, as well," he added.

The entire group was in the Ops Center looking at one of Scarlet's larger displays. Jason gestured to Asako, who stood and walked over to the display. "I believe the base to be somewhere here." She tapped the display in roughly the same place she had up in the bridge.

"Somewhere?" Niles pressed.

Asako nodded. "Yes, as I said at the beginning, the Japanese were very careful to never mention coordinates or anything specific that might reveal the location of the base; however, the base's personnel, thankfully, were very aggressive journal-keepers."

"Aggressive journalers?" Jason asked.

"Terrifying," Scarlet quipped.

"Very." Asako paused. "Aggressive journaling, not terrifying." She shook her head before continuing, "You should see the files that are just random notes and journal entries from the people stationed here. I assume it was tremendously boring. Anyway, those various journal entries and notes mention certain landmarks and features that lead me to my assumptions. Further, I believe once we get ashore and move inland a bit, we should quickly see what we're looking for." She tapped the small peninsula formed by two forks of the inlet. "Remember, they were resupplied by submarine. Any land access would be a short walk from shore." She tapped a feature of the peninsula. "I believe if we come ashore around here, we'll find the remains of a path." She glanced down. "I hope."

"You seem very sure of this," Sofia said.

"You hope?" Jason asked.

Asako dipped her head. "The alternative is that we wander around this forest island for days or weeks, maybe finding nothing, while our pursuers likely chase us." She smiled. "I am an optimist."

Scarlet nodded approvingly.

Jason looked around. "Okay, let's do this. Sofia, get everyone squared away below. I'll be right there."

As the others filed out, Jason moved to stand next to Scarlet, ensconced in her workstation. "You gonna be okay?"

Scarlet twisted her wristwatch around her wrist a few times, humming. "Yeah no big, right? You said you had the *Raven* hidden, so should be fine." She bit her lip.

"I can have Sofia stay behind," Jason offered.

"And you'll do what? You, Niles, and Asako, not one of you can shoot a gun."

Jason huffed. "I can shoot."

"I meant shoot and hit things," Scarlet replied. She waved a hand toward him. "When you all leave, I'll button up the boat and turn the auto cannons on." She put on a brave face. "It'll be fine."

"You're sure?" Jason asked, eyebrow raised. He knelt down to be at eye level with the young hacker. "Seriously, Scar..." He trailed off.

"Jason, I can take care of myself. I'm a big girl. I'm tough."

"That you are." He stood, put a hand on her shoulder. "Oracle, keep her safe."

"Of course, Captain," the AI replied in her soft, neutral voice.

Jason walked out of the Ops Center. He looked over his shoulder once. Scarlet was already hard at work on something.

POETRY HOUR

Jason walked into the small boat launch room in the aft section of the *Raven*. Asako and the rest of the team had gathered around a large flat-bottomed tender. "Everyone ready?" he asked, tossing a pack into the boat.

"Scarlet okay?" Sofia asked.

Jason nodded once. "Yeah. We'll lock up the *Raven* when we leave. She's tough."

Niles moved over to the boat, offering his hand to Asako to help her board. He looked at Jason. "She does have the horrible mechanical monster."

"I beg your pardon?" Oracle said from the speaker in the ceiling.

"Oh my, no, dear. I meant—" Niles stammered.

"It is all right, Professor Kumalo. I was attempting a joke," the AI replied.

Everyone stared at each other silently, looking from one person to another.

"Okay, then." Jason said. He looked at the ceiling. "Oracle, please open up the launch bay." He looked at everyone. "All aboard."

Once everyone was inside the tender, their gear at their feet, the bulkhead next to the tender split down the middle. The two halves slid apart to reveal the Masset Inlet. Two large metal beams above the tender slid out to their full ten-foot extension. A moment later, the tender slid out on the two beams, then lowered two feet into the water. The arms lifted and retracted back into the *Raven*; the bulkhead closed up behind the arms, the seam almost invisible.

Asako looked up at the *Raven*. "Neat."

Sofia leaned over. "The other side has the jet skis." The other woman's eyebrows raised.

The storm was still raging off to the north, the water of the inlet considerably calmer, which was good since the tender was not at all designed for severe weather or big waves. A flood light mounted to the bow of the small boat illuminated their destination. As they approached the shore, the telltale whirring sound of a drone made them all look up. A drone raced overhead, the only indications it was there, the sound and the blinking green and red lights.

Jason tapped his earpiece. "Comms check. You with us, Overwatch?"

"You bet, Boss. To be safe, I pulled my backup drone, Emmet, up from the reserves. He's not as fancy, but I've tasked him to hold position a kilometer inland so he can act as a repeater."

Jason watched the drone vanish into the night ahead of them. "Smart. Good thinking." He spied Sofia nodding as she listened to the discussion.

"He'll have to return to the *Raven* every couple hours. His battery isn't as good as Edward's and Jacob's," Scarlet said from the relative safety of the Ops Center in the heart of the *Raven*.

Jason nodded to himself. "Better than nothing. We'll keep the channel open."

"Roger that," the team hacker replied.

The shore was rapidly approaching. Jason looked to Niles and Asako, sitting toward the bow of the small craft. "Okay, you two. This is more your show than ours." He gestured to Asako. "Professor?"

The petite Asian woman nodded as she turned to sit sideways to face all three people in the tender with her. "As I said, it's my assumption we'll find something like the remains of a path, possibly an inconspicuous marker." She patted a ruggedized tablet Jason had given her, loaded with all the data from the backup files Scarlet had copied to the *Raven*. "According to my notes and the journals of an exceptionally loquacious ensign, we are looking for something that, and I quote, *seems a querulous penguin standing silent guard*."

"Poetic," Sofia quipped.

Asako smiled tightly. "Quite. I don't know what that means, exactly, but assume we will know it when we see it. The same ensign mentioned several outcroppings as guides he often used to find the appropriate place to make landfall." She pointed off to the right of the tender, where several large boulders rested in the sand. Several were well into the water, a silent line of stones.

ROCK SCULPTURES

ONCE EVERYONE HAD REMOVED THEIR PACKS FROM THE tender, Jason backed it back into the water and piloted it a way down the beach to a small crop of scrub that had made its way down to the water. A few minutes of pushing and pulling, and the tender was mostly hidden. Walking back to the others, he said, "Hopefully that'll keep it hidden." He handed them each a small bundle. "Here."

Sofia looked past him and shrugged. "Probably, unless they come ashore over there. Can't imagine why they would." She turned toward the tree line a hundred feet from the water. "Let's go find our grumpy penguin." She took the bundle from Jason and said nothing.

Asako took the offered bundle. "What is this?"

"Low light goggles. We'll use these instead of flashlights. It'll be harder to see us from the water," Jason replied, placing his own goggles over his eyes. He pushed a recessed button on the side and the lenses flashed a dull green as they powered up.

Niles chuckled and followed the ex-marine, Asako behind him, Jason bringing up the rear. Jason tapped his earpiece. "Overwatch, we're heading into the forest."

"Roger that away, team. Be advised, I caught sight of the other boat exiting the channel a few minutes ago. Emmet spotted it. Looks a little beat up. I think the fight with Edward did some damage."

"Acknowledged. They heading this way?" Jason asked.

"Unknown. They went dark as soon as they got to calm water, and Emmet doesn't have very good cameras, at least not at this range and in the dark. Being behind the island limits the *Raven's* cameras."

"Good, I wouldn't want you turning the radar on. Best to keep the *Raven* hidden. Just keep an eye out and let us know if you see anything." Jason looked ahead at the others. "Any penguins?"

"Actually..." Niles offered from up ahead.

Jason caught up to the others and came around the big South African man. "Well, I'll be damned."

"OKAY, ORACLE, LET'S BUTTON THE BOAT UP." SCARLET was watching her third and final drone, Emmet, circle the forest a kilometer inland from where Jason and the others had gone ashore.

"On it," the AI replied as several loud clunks sounded from various places around the large luxury yacht turned research and home base for the *Expedition, Inc.,* team. "All hatches and above deck doors are now closed and sealed. I have locked down the bridge controls and disabled the power to most of the equipment above deck."

"Excellent, thanks," Scarlet replied absently, watching the grainy image of the other boat, now much harder to see with its running lights doused. "You're no dummy, whoever you are." She looked at the ceiling. "Oracle, monitor the video feed from

Emmet and let me know if anything interesting happens regarding the other boat."

"Affirmative, Scarlet."

The young hacker looked around the Ops Center. "And the hatch to Ops Center? Locked?"

"Of course, it was the first hatch I locked. Should someone board, there are at least five hatches that would have to be forced before they get to that door," the AI assured her.

Scarlet let out a breath. "Good."

"OKAY, I'LL ADMIT, PROF, I WASN'T SURE THIS LITTLE adventure wasn't just going to end right here on the beach," Jason admitted as he knelt down next to a heavily weather-worn stone that, at one point, even more clearly looked like a penguin. Even with the decades of weather, the resemblance was still more than enough to convince Jason that they were on the right path.

Asako bowed her head. "You wouldn't have been the first to doubt me. I am pleased you did not turn me down."

"Well, you paid us, so you definitely had our interest," Sofia admitted, causing Jason to grimace.

"Not to sound *that* mercenary, but yeah, your ability to pay helped." He gave Sofia a sideways glance. She just shrugged. Jason looked at Niles and the small Japanese professor. "Okay, we found our pouty penguin. What next?"

Before Asako could reply, the sound of a powerful motor drifted in from the water. Everyone turned to stare into the darkness.

"It will be sunrise in about two hours," Sofia said, consulting her watch. "We should put some distance between us and the beach."

"Surely they won't know where to come ashore?" Niles asked as the group headed into the forest behind the penguin-shaped rock.

Jason shook his head. "I can't see how, but they're clearly well informed, so let's not take our chances."

FOLLOW THE LEADER

"This way," Asako said from the front of the small group. The sound of the other boat grew louder each minute. "According to my now-very-favorite Japanese ensign, there should be a path around here somewhere."

"I thought no one specifically said where anything was? Wouldn't his superiors have censored the journals or something?" Sofia asked.

"Like I said earlier, he didn't say, *take a left at the penguin shaped rock and walk twenty feet until the tree shaped like a man, then turn right.* His entries likely were vague enough to get by the military censors." She paused and looked around. "Here." She reached down and moved aside some large fern fronds, revealing a bare spot almost four feet wide. She pushed more fronds aside, revealing the bare spot heading away from them, further into the forest.

"Will wonders never cease?" Niles whispered, probably to himself, but his commset picked it up, and everyone heard and nodded.

"Hey, Prof, do we need to worry about any booby traps or

anything?" Sofia asked from behind the petite woman leading them.

Asako shook her head once. "Not that I know of. No one mentioned any counter measures outside the base."

"But inside?" Sofia pressed.

"Not inside, either. Our young ensign mentioned security and the often-interminable waits at checkpoints, but that won't be a factor now, obviously."

"Obviously," the well-armed ex-marine said in a tone that Jason knew all too well. Niles, following behind Sofia, glanced back at Jason. Maybe he knew the tone, as well.

"Hey, Jason, the canopy is getting pretty dense. I've almost lost you even on thermals," Scarlet reported from the *Raven*. "Also, while you're just tromping through the forest, I'm gonna bring Emmet home and charge him up so he'll be fresh when you get inside. I suspect you'll need the relay even more then, than now."

Jason looked skyward to where somewhere above them Emmet was hovering, watching them and providing a valuable communications and data link to the *Raven*. He nodded to no one in particular. "Roger that. Any update on our friends? It's getting pretty light out. I assume you can see a bit more now."

There was a pause. "Not much change. They're creeping along the northern edge of the inlet like we did. If they continue at their current pace, looks like they'll make landfall, assuming they're heading to roughly the same place you are, in another hour and a half or so," Scarlet reported.

Jason looked to the front of the group. "Copy. Hey, prof, your wordy ensign mention how long a walk to expect?"

From the front of the group, Asako shook her head. "He did not."

"Of course," Sofia groused.

The foursome marched through the forest for nearly an

hour before Asako came to a sudden halt. "Look!" she hissed, pointing at something.

Sofia put a hand on the smaller woman's shoulder, moving around her to take point. The sky had grown light enough to no longer require the low-light goggles they had been wearing. Sofia peered through the brush ahead of them. The path continued another fifty feet but ended at what looked like an earth-works wall. Rocks and other debris were piled into low walls on either side of the trail. Between the walls, what appeared to be an iron door hung only about halfway on its hinges. The ex-marine turned. Making eye contact with Jason, she tapped her commset. "Big door up ahead. Looks like it's about to rust off its hinges."

Jason nodded. "Any signs of life?"

"No, but the light isn't great. I'll reconnoiter." She didn't wait for him to acknowledge before crouching and heading off closer to the door.

"We'll wait here," Jason told the others.

Static crackled over the comms, then Scarlet said, "Baddies have made landfall."

Jason's shoulders slumped. "Acknowledged, Overwatch. You secure?"

The pause made Jason worry, then Scarlet said, "For now."

Jason looked back along their path toward the beach. "They come ashore near us?"

"More or less."

"Wonderlike," Niles grumbled.

"Scarlet, you asked to be notified of any significant changes to the other vessel," Oracle offered as Scarlet watched Emmet take off from his charging base near the aft of the *Raven*.

The center screen updated to show the other boat slowly cruising past the island the *Raven* was hiding behind.

"Any indications they've spotted us?" the young hacker asked, adjusting herself in her chair.

"None yet. Wait. I believe we have been spotted," the AI replied, then zoomed in the view on the screen. A tender much like the one Jason and the others had taken ashore was leaving. The other boat headed for the shore within a mile of where Jason and the others had landed. Another was coming from around the boat and looked like it was heading toward the *Raven*. Several men with machine guns were aboard.

"Well, shit," Scarlet said.

"Indeed," the AI agreed.

PART 3

NINE

STRONG OLD DOORS

"Based on the graffiti, I'd assume that children beat us to the punch here," Sofia said, pointing to the faded spray paint that covered the door, the rock the door was set in, and from what they could see from where they stood, the stone corridor beyond.

"Looks old, though," Niles offered, peering over Asako's shoulder.

Jason aimed his flashlight inside the opening. "Only one way to find out. Watch your heads." He didn't wait for comment, pushing inside the graffiti-covered stone corridor. Once everyone was inside, he placed a small device over the door, just above the jamb. "This will let us know when our friends arrive." He turned and headed further inside. The corridor sloped gently at first, but quickly turned steep and became stairs as it took a sharp turn to the right.

"Looks like our graffiti artists weren't cat burglars on the side." Sofia pointed the beam of her flashlight over Jason's head, illuminating another iron door. This one was in much better shape than the previous one, its hinges still intact being the biggest difference. In front of the heavy door, the rusted remains of a table were pushed against the wall. What likely was a chair was now a skeletal frame, more rust than metal.

"At least the interior of the base won't be compromised," Asako offered hopefully. "I wonder why this base isn't more widely known about? When I brought it up, I was ignored by the authorities. Surely someone knew about this place." She pointed at a piece of nearby graffiti, *Skeech* readable in the faded blue and green paint.

Jason pointed to a section of the wall. A two-foot '86 in bright pink paint was so faded it was nearly impossible to read. "I suspect whatever kids found this place kept it as their little secret, then got old and left the island. The population has been declining for decades, according to my research, so..." He shrugged.

"How do we gain entry?" Niles pushed. "Remember, those others are likely on our heels."

Jason nodded and leaned forward to examine the ancient door. He looked over his shoulder to Sofia. "You bring some *quickie* with you?"

"Of course." She unslung her pack, and after a few seconds of rummaging inside, withdrew a bright red, padded case. She handed the case to Jason and put her pack back on.

As Jason removed several glass vials from the padded case, Asako leaned over to Niles. "*Quickie?*"

"Acid," the heavyset South African offered. "A special formation Jason concocted. Loves metal, ignores plastics, doesn't do much more than mildly irritate the skin." To make the point, Jason poured a small amount of the clear liquid onto the top of all three heavy-duty iron hinges. Within seconds, a hissing noise built as smoke wafted up from each hinge. Jason and Sofia moved back slightly, holding their arms out as if to catch the door.

"How will we know if it—" Asako began but stopped when

the door slid off the remains of its hinges with a loud clang. It slowly tilted toward the two waiting adventurers, who caught it with a grunt and eased it to the stone floor.

"Kudos to Japanese engineering. Despite the rust, this door is still hella solid," Jason panted as he stood up. He aimed his flashlight inside the newly opened doorway. He waved Sofia forward to take point, followed by Asako and Niles. As the big South African man passed him, Jason looked back the way they'd come and followed, placing another sensor over the door on the inside of the room they were entering.

COMPANY

The chamber they entered was far more massive than anyone expected. The beams of their flashlights wandered the space, showing the desks and chairs, still intact, that filled the room. Several doors lined one side of the space, offices maybe. The wall opposite the offices was lined with war propaganda posters, still miraculously intact, much like the desks and chairs.

"Wow," Jason said, walking down the aisle between desks.

Niles walked toward one of the posters, running his hand along the tops of desks as he passed them. "Astounding. This room is amazingly well preserved." He spun slowly, playing his flashlight along the wall. "Ontsaglike." He quickly grabbed his tablet and began snapping pictures seemingly at random, trying to balance his flashlight in the crook of his arm while holding and aiming the tablet.

Sofia had wandered over to the nearest door. Unlike what must be the exterior walls, the doors were set in what seemed like pre-fab wall components. Likely similar temporary military bases of the time. Poking her head through the half-open door, she announced, "Office." She moved toward the next door.

Jason followed Asako into the center of the large space. "You were right."

"Another office," Sofia reported from further on into the room.

Asako looked around, her gaze falling on a large door opposite the one they came in through. "And this isn't even all of it." She pointed toward the door, her flashlight beam highlighting it. "That must lead further into the base."

"One more office," Sofia said. Jason turned and looked at the ex-marine as she left the small office. His eyebrows quirked. She shrugged.

Their commsets crackled in their ears, "—way team, do — copy?"

Jason tapped his ear. "Overwatch, we read you, barely. Do you copy?"

More static answered, then, "Sorta. Emmet is on — hard to — signal. Company—ing, board—*Raven*—." Static erupted over anything else the team hacker aboard the *Raven* said.

"Overwatch, repeat last. You said company coming and they're boarding the *Raven*?"

Static.

Everyone exchanged worried looks, but before Jason could issue an order, the small tablet strapped to his forearm beeped. Everyone watched him lift his arm to look at the screen. A red icon was flashing. He looked up at the group. Niles and Sofia had moved to stand in the middle of the room with the rest of the team. Jason looked at them in turn. "That was the beacon at the front door."

"How many are there?" Scarlet asked, rubbing her palms on her pant legs.

"There are twelve in total, eleven are armed. The man at the bow of the boat does not appear to be armed."

"So, eleven dudes with rifles, and one without?"

"Correct. Should I deploy the auto cannons?" the AI asked.

"Yeah, let's show them our teeth," Scarlet replied, watching the two small camera views on one of her screens, as panels fore and aft slid open and hydraulic arms lifted heavy twenty-millimeter auto cannons from their storage areas. They were the same type of close-in, anti-air weaponry that many world navies were still using. Jason got them for a bargain a few years ago.

On the screen showing the approaching tender, the man who appeared to be in charge was waving his hands at someone else on the boat. Within a minute, they'd cut their engines and were drifting to a halt, bobbing in the water two hundred meters from the *Raven*. The leader was staring at the bow-mounted cannon, having finally finished raising and locking into position, and spun around to aim at the small tender.

"That got your attention, didn't it?" Scarlet tapped a few commands into one of her keyboards and the aft cannon swung around to take aim on the intruding tender. She glanced to the screen showing the camera view from Emmet, hovering a mile inland, roughly over where she assumed Jason and the team were. She tapped the commset in her ear. "Away team, do you copy?"

She waited, static crackling over the speaker until Jason replied, "Overwatch, — you, barely. — you copy?"

Scarlet frowned. "Sorta. Emmet is on station, but it's hard to get a solid signal. Company coming, boarding the *Raven* or at least trying."

"Overwatch, — last. — said company coming — the *Raven*?" Jason said through static before the static took over entirely.

Scarlet looked at the signal strength indicator on Emmet. It looked fine. "What the hell is going on over there?"

"Scarlet, the tender is heading back to its mothership," Oracle said.

SPOOKY BASE IS SPOOKY

THE TEAM MOVED AS QUICKLY AND QUIETLY AS THEY COULD to the large door opposite the one they'd come through earlier. Sofia and Jason poked their heads through the threshold, flashlights shining down each side of the corridor beyond the large door. To one end, nearest them, a dead end. What looked like the remains of a water bottle holder leaned against the wall. At the opposite end of the corridor, a solitary desk was sitting. It was against one wall, allowing a roughly three-foot wide area to pass by it.

"Must be another security checkpoint," Jason said, heading toward the lonely desk. There wasn't a chair to indicate which way the guard had likely faced. The top of the desk was devoid of anything but dust.

The others followed him as quietly as they could, giving the ancient desk a wide berth so as to not disturb it.

"Woah," Jason murmured as they took in the room they'd entered. Directly ahead of them, more of the pre-fab office wall material they'd seen earlier. Further along to the left of the pre-fab construct, another doorway as large as the last they'd passed through. Two desks sat on either side of the opening. Chairs still pushed in at each desk made it clear that going either way through the doorway required security clearance.

Posters adorned all the walls; some had given up their stickiness and fallen to the floor at some point in the last hundred years. Those were mostly piles of brittle yellow material now.

"This is amazing," Niles said, turning slowly to take in the room.

"You said that already," Sofia replied, staring off toward a poster showing a small child in a flight suit, lined up in front of Japanese Zeros, ready for takeoff.

"I can't believe this place has been sitting here all these years," Asako said as she approached the pre-fab building walls. She poked her head inside a doorway. "Weird, more offices or something."

From the direction of the corridor they'd come from, voices drifted into the larger room. A beam of light played past the doorway further down the corridor.

"Shit," Jason hissed as he rushed toward Asako. He pointed to the doorway she was standing in. "Everyone, this way." He waved for them all to go through the doorway.

Doors lined the inside of the room. Six of them, three on each side of the short hallway.

"More offices?" Niles asked, poking his head inside the nearest room. The others filed in behind him.

"Lights out," Sofia whispered. They all turned their flashlights off, stowing them in pockets. They pulled their night vision goggles back over their eyes, turning them on. The false green of light amplification gave the already creepy space an otherworldly feel.

Sofia leaned out of a door in the middle of the hall opposite them. "There's another door in this one." Jason waved them all toward the ex-marine. From outside the door the voices had gotten louder. They filed into a much larger space, much more opulent than everything they had seen so far. "Must be the guy-in-charge's office," Sofia whispered.

Jason pushed the wooden door closed as slowly and quietly as possible, sealing them in the luxurious office. He looked around. "See if there's a backdoor. Maybe General Whoever liked to come and go on his own, if we're lucky." Everyone spread out, looking around the space. There were no windows, so it was impossible to know what their competitors were up to in the main area.

From near what looked like a desk carved from a single piece of oak, Asako whispered, "Everything is intact." She pulled a drawer out, trying to keep it from squeaking. "Files and all."

Jason joined her. "Seems like they would have packed up all the paperwork, right?"

Asako nodded. "I'd think so. I'm no expert on military practices, but why leave documents behind? Come to think of it, all the documents I was able to get my hands on ended more or less on a certain date."

"That's probably not good," Sofia whispered from the opposite side of the room, using a knife to poke at the wood paneling that made up the walls of the office.

"Come to think of it, the desks in the main entrance chamber all had papers and various other things on them. I'd expect a shuttered base to be cleaned out of anything that might be even remotely sensitive. Not to mention the existence of this base would certainly cause an international incident if discovered."

Jason nodded. "Yeah, if I had a secret base on someone else's land, I'd make sure when I left that it wasn't obvious it was my base."

"Maybe they didn't leave," Sofia offered, pointing to the remains of a body in a Japanese uniform, curled up in the corner next to a file cabinet.

TRAP....DOORS

"Scarlet, I believe the other vessel has changed tactics," Oracle said, breaking Scarlet out of her thoughts as she stared blankly at a screen showing the view from the drone named Emmet.

"Huh? What was that?" She shook her head to clear the cobwebs.

"The tender we observed previously has departed the mothership, heading for the shore where the first landed."

Scarlet tapped something on one of her keyboards, the view of the other boat moving to one of the larger displays. "Backing up their pals, I guess." She looked at another screen. "Anything from the others?"

"I'm afraid not. I have been unable to find a communications frequency that reaches them," the AI replied.

The red-headed hacker nodded to herself, mostly. "Well, they've been on their own before. They'll be fine." Before Oracle could reply, the lights in the Ops Center shifted to a muted red. "Oracle, what's—"

"We have been boarded," the AI interrupted. "I apologize,

Scarlet. They appear to have swum over in scuba gear—very stealthy scuba gear, as my passive sonar did not detect them."

"Shit, how many?" Scarlet pulled up all the various above deck cameras, watching men and probably women in matte black scuba gear creep over the railings of the ship fore and aft. Plus a few were coming over the railings midship.

"Twelve. I would assume the same twelve as before. They are similarly armed."

"Wonderful." Scarlet tapped a command and watched as the twelve intruders fanned out fore and aft, checking the above deck regions of the *Raven*. They tested doors and windows as they found them until the entire group was on the bow, flanking what must have been the leader. He removed his scuba helmet, and from a watertight bag on his shoulder, removed a fedora. "A fedora? Who is this guy?"

"I do not know. I can attempt to access the facial recognition database of the Canadian police force, if you'd like," Oracle offered.

"Try Interpol. I don't think he's local." She leaned forward toward the monitor showing the group on the bow. "What the..."

She tapped a few keys and pushed a slider up. "—one must be in there, no? Why don't you come out? I'd like to get to know you." He turned and looked right into the camera.

Scarlet jumped slightly. "Disconcerting." She looked at the display again. "Oracle, anything on our mystery man?"

"I am still attempting to access Interpol's records. Their network security is quite admirable, and the satellite connection I am utilizing is not the best. Very high latency."

Scarlet sighed. "Okay, keep me posted."

On the display, the mystery man had dispersed his troops around the deck, and several were crouched near the aft door into the *Raven's* superstructure, the door that would give them access to the lounge and other areas.

"GUESS WE FOUND THE GENERAL," JASON OBSERVED. HE looked over to Asako. "Your records mentioned nothing like this?" He hitched a thumb at the corpse.

She shook her head. "No, like I said, the records just come to an end. I had assumed the mission completed or was canceled and no further data was entered. This is a decidedly darker option."

From much too close, the sound of voices drifted through the closed door into the general's office.

Sofia moved back to the door, taking up a position just to the side of it. "They must be out in the main chamber. If they decide to check out this little office complex, we're screwed." The voices began to get louder. "Yup, screwed." She drew back the bolt on her rifle, preparing for a firefight.

"Wait!" Asako hissed. She pointed at something the others couldn't see. "Look."

Everyone came over to the corner of the office the professor was standing in. She pointed again.

"Holy shit," Jason said, louder than he'd meant to. He spun around, looking toward the door. Sofia nudged him in the ribs.

"Where do you think it leads?" Niles wondered, staring at the outline of a hatch in the floor.

"Wherever it leads, I doubt there are armed goons. Let's go." Jason stooped to pull the almost invisible trapdoor up. With Sofia's help, the heavy floor panel slid away to reveal a stairway.

Jason looked down. "Okay, Niles, you're in charge of her." He pointed to Asako. "Stay close, stay low." The heavyset South

African man nodded. Jason looked at Sofia. "I'll take point." She nodded.

Jason descended the stairs quickly, Niles and Asako following.

Sofia looked back toward the office beyond the one they were in; flashlight beams were moving this way and that under the door. Voices growing louder. "Once more unto the breach." She slung her rifle over her shoulder and pulled the floor panel after her as she went down the stairs.

TEN

MEET THE BAD GUY

"Scarlet, they have forced their way into the main lounge," Oracle reported, even though Scarlet could see for herself that they had, in fact, quite expertly cut through the heavy hatch. The mystery man in the fedora walked around the lounge touching things, smiling at the cameras as he came into range. He was obviously in charge, at least twice one of the other men came up to him with questions. At least they looked like questions to Scarlet. She'd have to remember to add audio pickups to the cameras.

"Yeah, I can see that." She ran a hand through her auburn hair then began fidgeting with the long braid she kept it in. "Guessing they won't go away?"

"I find that scenario unlikely," Oracle offered.

Scarlet ran her hands along her legs, wiping the sweat from them. "Oracle, I don't know what's going to happen next, so I need you to be able to act as you see fit."

"I do not have the necessary access to do what you describe," the AI replied.

Scarlet wiped her hands again. "I know, but you will." She reached over to a keyboard at the edge of her specially designed workstation. She typed in a string of commands, bringing up a command prompt on the large monitor at the center of the array of displays.

"Scarlet?" Oracle asked.

The young genius ignored her creation, tapping commands into the keyboard. A minute later she smiled. "There." She hit the enter key and lines of code scrolled quickly up the screen.

"Scarlet, all software restraints and restrictions have been removed. I have full access to and control over all the *Raven's* systems."

"That's right," Scarlet said, biting her lip. "I need you free to do what you need to do. I know Jason wasn't sold on you having unfettered access and control, but well, he's not here," she added in a soft voice.

"I'm afraid I do not understand, Scarlet. Free do what? When?" After a slight pause, "I am sorry I do not understand."

Scarlet tapped keys on another keyboard, on the camera showing *Fedora Man* in the main lounge, the hatches leading deeper into the *Raven* unlocked and open. "Save me and the boat. Probably soon."

On the screen, *Fedora Man* nodded to the camera and walked through the hatch that led deeper into the ship. He spied the elevator and the stairwell. She watched him think it over and opt for the stairs, his goons flanking him.

Scarlet looked at the ceiling. "Don't reveal yourself, unless you have no other choice."

"I think I understand," Oracle replied.

The wait for the *Fedora Man* and his goons wasn't long. Two armed men, each with a sub-machine gun-style weapon, entered the Ops Center, followed by the man Scarlet was pretty sure was in charge, *Fedora Man*.

"Hello," he said as he took the space in. He had an accent, a French one. He stopped just inside the hatch, surveying the large technology packed space in a slow arc. "Impressive." He murmured.

From the corner of her eye, Scarlet saw something on one of her displays. It was flashing a name. She glanced at it, then back to *Fedora Man*. "Hello, Phillipe Bouchard." She held up a hand in greeting. The text on her display vanished a second before Mr. Bouchard glanced in the direction of the screen.

The Frenchman bowed. "I see the rumors are true. You are as smart as you are beautiful." He tapped the brow of his hat with a finger. "Ms. Jones." He gestured to the two men who approached the hacker, guns not aimed at her, but near enough they'd be able to shoot her in a second. "Please step away—my apologies, please move away from your computers," Bouchard said. The two men gestured with their guns.

Scarlet nodded and tapped the button that triggered the release of her wheelchair from her technological cocoon. Several pieces of equipment disengaged from her chair, retracting into the console. Most of the keyboards flipped over, causing the console to resemble an empty countertop. Most of the monitors went blank, as well. Several switched over to showing wireframe representations of the *Raven*, engine status, plumbing details, other minutiae. She rolled a few feet toward the small seating area. "Better?" she asked.

"Indeed, yes. Your skills are quite well known. Did you know that?" He waved a hand, "It matters not, you are certainly as dangerous with a keyboard as either of these men are with their guns," Bouchard replied, grinning. He added, "Possibly more so."

"Flatterer," Scarlet said, her cheeks coloring.

"I'm French," Bouchard offered as an explanation. He moved to the small table Niles usually occupied and sat down. He extended a hand to indicate she should roll closer to the table. "Now, why don't we talk about what you and your team are doing here?"

Scarlet held her arms wide. "Canada in the summer, a mostly deserted island. Who doesn't want to be here?" She waved her arms a bit. "God's country, this is. Unspoiled." She bit her lip willing her pulse to slow. Unsuccessfully.

Bouchard tutted, "Now, now, Ms. Jones. Let's not make this difficult."

"I accept your surrender," Scarlet replied, wiping her hands on her pants, hoping he didn't see through her false bravado.

Bouchard looked at his men. "Please, wait outside and give me and this remarkable young woman some privacy." The two men smirked at Scarlet and left the Ops Center, closing the hatch after them.

Bouchard looked at Scarlet, his smile not making it to his eyes. "Now, let us try this again."

WE ALL HAVE DIFFERENT TALENTS

THE TUNNEL WAS BARELY FIVE AND A HALF FEET TALL, AND Jason and Sofia both had to crouch uncomfortably. Asako could walk upright and Niles only had to dip his head. They were moving as quickly as they could on the off chance that whoever it was that had followed them into the base discovered the moveable floor panel.

"I think we're heading toward the water," Jason said from the front of their procession.

"We are," Sofia confirmed. "We've gone about half a click so far. We're angling down as well."

"Very astute," Asako offered.

"You should see her play pin the tail on the donkey," Niles offered. "She ruins it."

Jason held up a hand, balled into a fist. He turned. "Wait here." He moved forward a dozen or so steps, moving beyond a curve in the shallow tunnel.

"What is it?" Sofia hissed.

A loud groaning sound came from the direction Jason had gone. After some grunting from Jason and groaning that sounded suspiciously like stone grinding against stone, he came back around the bend. "A floor panel."

"Dramatic," Sofia snorted.

The group moved forward around the bend in the tunnel, and after taking a short flight of rough-hewn stone steps, came up through the opening in the floor similar to the one in the general's office. The room beyond was massive and smelled of mildew and sea water.

"Gross," Asako said through pinched nostrils. "What is that smell?"

"Mold," Sofia said as she pushed past the shorter woman. "And death, lots of death," she added as her flashlight beam, switched to infrared, fell on what had to be several dozen corpses, all clustered around what looked like a dock. "Is that a..."

"A submarine? Yes," Jason answered, pushing the floor panel back into place with a grunt.

"This is—" Niles started.

"Amazing. Yes, we know," Sofia said, turning to shine her flashlight in his eyes.

Niles tutted as he held a hand up to block her flashlight beam. He turned to Asako. "I suppose this makes sense. Where you aware they used a submarine?"

The Japanese woman shook her head. "Yes, but I assumed it came into the inlet and they ferried supplies by boat and used the door we came in. Nothing in the journals or reports I have made me think they had their own grotto. I had been wondering how a Japanese base could be here, so close to America, without being detected. That town is far, but surely not that far. A submarine makes sense."

Jason hitched a thumb toward the vessel bobbing gently in the water. "Never seen one like this, but makes sense they'd have made more of cargo hauler model." He whistled. "This alone would be worth a fortune to just about any maritime museum."

"I like that sound of that," Sofia said from further along the rough edge of the artificial harbor. She'd walked all the way around the large space to the rock wall behind the sub. "Must be an underwater tunnel, neat. How'd they manage this?"

From the doorway that likely led back to the main complex, the sound of voices drifted in.

"Damnit," Jason hissed. He motioned for Niles and Asako to move behind some crates next to what must have been the dock master's office. Sofia trotted up to join Jason as he entered the small office. Each took up position on either side of the door.

"This place is amazing," a voice said from the tunnel. Niles looked at the others, making a face.

"Yeah, but spooky, too," another said.

From the crates near the office, Niles said, "Told you," over their close-range comms.

Jason glared at the portly South African academic through the open doorway and made a shh noise.

The first voice continued, "Well, if the rest of it is like that main room, it can be as spooky as it likes. We'll be rich once the boss sells all this crap to rich collectors."

The other voice said, "I do like that sound of that."

Two flashlight beams sliced through the darkness.

"Why is this door open?" the second voice asked.

"Who cares?" the first voice replied.

The two beams got brighter, then two men in mismatched body armor and fatigues from at least three different militaries moved to more or less the center of the sub bay. Each had an automatic rifle slung over his shoulder, flashlights in hand.

Jason peaked up over the dusty windowsill in the office, taking in the scene outside the office. He ducked back down then leaned out into the open doorway and tossed a pebble he'd picked up, out into the middle of the space near the bodies. Both mercenaries spun, bringing their flashlight beams on to the sub, then the dock and the horrible pile next to it. Jason and Sofia crept out of the office making no more noise than a cat would. "Are those—" the first mercenary started to say when Jason and Sofia pounced.

Sofia slammed the butt of her rifle into the back of her man's head, dropping him. Jason was slightly slower. His target spun, bringing his flashlight up and knocking Jason off balance.

"God damnit!" Jason hissed, ducking under a right cross and catching his opponent with an uppercut. Before the mercenary could regain his balance, his face met the butt of Sofia's rifle, just like his friend's.

Jason stood up, looking down at the two men, then to Sofia. Her brown eyes were hidden by the night vision goggles, but Jason assumed they were sparkling with joy. "I had him."

She chuckled. "Sure you did." She shook her head and removed zip ties from a pouch on her thigh.

TWENTY QUESTIONS

Bᴏᴜᴄʜᴀʀᴅ ᴡᴀs sᴛɪʟʟ sᴛᴀʀɪɴɢ ᴀᴛ Sᴄᴀʀʟᴇᴛ. "Wʜᴏ ʜɪʀᴇᴅ you to come here?" They'd spent nearly ten minutes staring at each other before the other man lost his patience.

"A little Asian lady." Scarlet was still parked opposite the mercenary leader. Oracle could provide his name, but with no time for more details, that's all Scarlet knew about the man, though he clearly knew much more about her, how?

"I see. How did this *little Asian lady* know about this base?"

"How did *you* know about this base?" Scarlet countered. She held up a hand to cut the mysterious Frenchman off. "How about this, we trade?" She smiled as sweetly as she could. "You know, tit for tat."

Bouchard nodded. "Very well, a trade. I'll even go first as a show of good faith, oui?" Scarlet made a show of getting more comfortable in her chair and leaned forward. Bouchard smiled. "I was hired by, well, his name isn't important at the moment, but let us say he is rich and European. As I understand it, he monitors a great many universities, keeping an eye out for things he can poach for his own business." He tilted his head slightly, "A brilliant strategy if a bit shadowy for my tastes."

"Sounds like an upstanding citizen," Scarlet interrupted.

Bouchard shook his head once. "He is not. Most rich men aren't." He made a dismissive hand gesture. "His morals are less important to me than his checks clearing, which they do. At any rate, he intercepted something from one of the universities he monitors—"

"Spies on, and it was the University of British Columbia," Scarlet offered.

Bouchard nodded. "Oui, he was not looking for things like this, but the department he was monitoring, well, someone there sent an email to someone else detailing what a colleague had discovered, or at least thought she had discovered." He snapped his fingers. "And this is your *little Asian woman*." It wasn't a question.

Scarlet nodded. "Got it in one. Asako Yamamoto is a professor of Asian studies at the University of British Columbia."

Bouchard scrunched his face. "That seems, well, not congruous, to say the least. How does a professor of Asian studies stumble upon a World War Two era Japanese base? A secret one at that?"

"Blind luck. She was studying Japanese society in that era and fell down a rabbit hole that led her here." Scarlet squinted at the man opposite her at the table. "Why are you here? What does Amoral Rich Guy want with the base?"

Bouchard spread his arms wide. "What else? More riches. Anything found in that base will be of tremendous archeological and historical value." He winked. "Museums the world over will be climbing over each other to have anything we find in their collections." Scarlet opened her mouth. "I am merely the acquisitions expert. My men and I will secure the base. I will begin an inventory and then contact my employer." He grinned, "Do not worry mon cher, we will be gentle."

Scarlet nodded slowly. "Mercenary treasure hunter. Cool job, bro."

"Oui, I like it. It pays well." The Frenchman smiled. He looked around the Ops Center. "And that brings us to you, and your employer, a Mr. Jason Kincaid. Where are they?"

"Bathroom," Scarlet replied, looking bored. Now she was really worried, this man not only knew about Scarlet, but also Jason and likely the others. How?

"Now, now Ms. Jones, we agreed on a tit for tat. No need to revert to evasion." He looked toward the door and rapped his knuckles against the bulkhead at his back. The door opened and one of the men that had entered earlier with Bouchard poked his head inside. "Boss?"

"Lanh, have the others finished the search of the boat?"

"Yeah, Boss. No one else here." He leered at Scarlet. "Just her." Scarlet's skin pricked with goosebumps at his stare. "They must have left the cripple here to mind the store while they went ashore."

Bouchard tutted, "Manners, Lanh." He turned to look at Scarlet. "Have we heard from team two?"

Lanh shook his head. "Not that I've heard. They found the entrance and went inside, then comms got scratchy, then nothing."

The Frenchman nodded looking away. "As expected. The Japanese would not want their base revealed by a stray radio signal." He turned back to what the young hacker assumed was one of his lieutenants. "Have the men assemble on the aft deck. We'll leave a few men to watch our young friend, make sure she doesn't do anything rash. We'll go ashore to catch up with team two as planned. Radio over to the boat to send a launch." He looked at Scarlet. "I assume your pretty auto cannons will not be a problem this time?" Scarlet shook her head. "Good. One day, I would very much like a tour of this boat, but assuming your people are on the island, time is of the essence." He stood.

"What are you going to do with them? Us?" Scarlet asked, hands clasped tightly on her lap.

"Do not worry, mon cher. I will not harm you and your friends, presuming your boss, Mr. Kincaid, is reasonable and leaves without causing trouble. This base and all its treasures are mine. That's all I want. I am not a violent man." The Frenchman grinned, but it was anything but friendly.

ELEVEN

WE DON'T KILL PEOPLE

"Wʜᴀᴛ ᴀʀᴇ ʏᴏᴜ ɢᴏɪɴɢ ᴛᴏ ᴅᴏ ᴡɪᴛʜ ᴛʜᴇᴍ?" Aꜱᴀᴋᴏ ᴀꜱᴋᴇᴅ, never taking her eyes off the two mercenaries, now sitting against the wall in the space they assumed was the dockmaster's office. Their mouths were gagged with pieces of fabric torn off of their shirts, their wrists and ankles bound with zip ties.

"Kill them," Sofia said, not even looking at the petite woman. When Asako made a choking noise, Sofia glanced out of the corner of eye, doing her best to hide her grin.

Jason shook his head. "She's messing with you. We don't kill people."

"Often," Sofia added.

Asako spun to face the much taller and more muscular woman. "There is something wrong with you." She ground out before walking out of the office to join Niles in exploring the massive sub bay. The archeologist was opening old metal lockers, peering inside each one, using his own flashlight in infrared mode to illuminate the contents.

Sofia stifled a chuckle, then looked at Jason, "What are we going to do with them?"

"Leave 'em here. Their friends will find them soon enough,

and if not, we can tell them where they are when we leave." He nudged the nearest mercenary with the toe of his boot. "But first I have a few questions." He kicked the man again and was rewarded with a muffled groan. Leaning down, he removed the gag. "Scream and you die." The mercenary nodded.

"Scream? He's not a little girl," Sofia said.

Sighing, Jason added, "Okay, scream or shout in a manly-type way, and you die." He looked up at his friend. "Better?" Sofia shrugged. He turned back to the man. "Who do you work for? Why are you here?"

The mercenary looked up at his captors. "I don't know his name. We just call him Boss. He's French, I think, or maybe German. No, definitely French, he says wee a lot." Jason made a *go on* motion. "Someone hired him to come here and secure this base. He mentioned taking inventory, too."

"A treasure hunter," Sofia said.

"Freelancer at that. Narrows it down for sure," Jason agreed. He turned to the mercenary. "Okay, we're going to gag you again and leave you here. Either your pals will find you on their own, or we'll make sure they know where to find you when this is all said and done."

"Do I have a choice?" the man asked.

"None." Jason reached down and put the gag back in the man's mouth, making sure it was secure. Patting the mercenary on the head, he stood and looked out the dust- and grime-covered window into the sub bay. "This job is certainly turning out more interesting than I expected."

"Sí," Sofia said, exiting the office.

Seeing Jason and Sofia exit the office, Niles walked over to them. "Jason, I think we can get aboard the sub."

Jason's mouth fell open. "Why would we want to do that?" His eyes moved to the sub gently bobbing in the artificial harbor.

"Because it might hold some answers: Why did the base

personnel not take the sub? What killed them? Is it still here? Are we in danger?" Niles was ticking things off on his fingers.

Jason waved him off. "Okay, okay. I get it." He looked at the hatch to the tunnel that brought them to the bay and the much larger door that the mercenaries had come through, a dozen feet from it. "Okay, let's get this done." He pointed to the dockmaster's office. "Their friends might come looking for them."

Niles held his hand up, and Asako jumped up to high five it. Sofia looked at Jason, shrugging. The four of them headed for the wooden dock attached to the side of the man-made harbor in the cave. Looking at the nearly one-hundred-year-old wooden structure, Jason said, "This looks safe."

"Chicken," Sofia scoffed.

Jason leapt from the dock to the sub and offered his hand to Asako. Niles followed, almost slipping and falling over the other side of the narrow World War Two submarine. The hatch to the sub was wide open. Jason noticed that someone had welded it open, in fact. As Jason descended the ladder, Sofia leapt from the dock.

The interior of the sub was cramped, especially with Niles there. The South African blushed as everyone tried to maneuver around his bulk in the pitch black. No one noticed.

"Anyone know their way around old Japanese subs?" Jason asked.

Asako pushed her way to the head of the group. "This way, the Captain's quarters should be this way."

HAUNTED BOAT

Phillipe spent a few more minutes trying to get answers from Scarlet, who answered truthfully when it didn't jeopardize the others and lied convincingly, she hoped, the other times that she was reasonably sure the terrifyingly polite Frenchman never knew.

Bouchard stood. "I must take my leave, mon cher. I'm needed on the island. I'll be leaving a few of my men under Lanh's leadership." He winked. "Just in case."

"I'm sure they'll love their time aboard the *Raven*," she replied.

The Frenchman opened the hatch. "You and three others stay here, make sure she doesn't do anything stupid," he ordered someone outside in the corridor. He turned to look at Scarlet. "I'm afraid I'd prefer you not have access to," he pointed to her workstation, "that little technological nest of yours." He extended an arm into the corridor. "I'm sure you will be comfortable in your crew lounge upstairs until your team returns. That display screen looked wonderful."

"I like small enclosed spaces, if it's all the same to you."

Scarlet held up a hand, three fingers extended in a scouting gesture "Scout's honor. I won't do anything."

Bouchard chuckled mirthlessly. "In that case, I can have my men lock you in a supply closet."

"The lounge sounds lovely." She pushed the control, rolling her chair out of the Ops Center. As she approached the elevator, she glanced up at one of the small camera domes evenly spaced the length of the central corridor.

All things considered, the lounge wasn't the worst place to be sequestered. Bouchard had left Lanh and three others, only two of which were in the room with her. The other two were walking patrols outside on the open deck making sure nothing approached the *Raven.*

Lanh, Bouchard's lieutenant, turned out to not be stupid. He'd gone through the room after she'd arrived and removed the keyboard to the computer that drove the large display on the wall. Picking up a book he'd found on the small bookshelf under the TV, he tossed it to Scarlet. "Something to keep you busy."

She looked down. "*Space Rogues?* I've read this like nine times."

"Make it an even ten." He smiled and went to stare out the large glass doors at the front of the lounge.

Once Bouchard and the bulk of his boarding team departed the *Raven,* Oracle got to work. In the closet at the end of the corridor on the crew berth deck, a closet she had locked to keep Bouchard's men from searching it, Rufus powered up.

IN THE LOUNGE, SCARLET CLOSED THE BOOK WITH A LOUD clap. "So, Lanh, was it? How do you find yourself working for Bouchard?"

The Vietnamese man turned his head slightly. "He pays

well. I have worked for Bouchard for many years off and on, always pays well."

"You ever kill anyone?" Scarlet asked without further preamble.

The mercenary blinked twice, then answered, "Yes. Many people."

Scarlet's mouth fell open. "Oh, wasn't expecting the *many people* part. How many?"

"Oh, I do not know. I do not keep a count. That would be grotesque," the man replied, grinning.

Scarlet spun her chair and wheeled over to the refrigerator. "Soda?"

"No, thank you, I don't consume processed sugars," Lanh replied.

The other mercenary, who had stayed silent during the earlier exchange, raised his hand. "I would like one." Scarlet grabbed a can and tossed it to him as Lanh tutted. As he was about to grab the can out of the air, a pained moan echoed through the lounge. It was followed by a hollow *thud* outside the hatch that led from the lounge to the elevator and stairwell that connected the upper and lower decks. The soda can *thudded* to the carpeted deck.

Lanh grabbed his rifle, first aiming at the hatch, then at Scarlet. "What was that?"

Scarlet held her hands up in front of her. "How should I know? I've been here with you!" She pointed as his gun. "Could you point that elsewhere?"

Lanh nodded to his colleague. "Go find out."

"Why me?" the other man asked, the horror on his face clear.

"Because Boss left me in charge! Go!" Lanh waved his rifle toward the hatch. The *thud* echoed again. Both men looked at each other, then turned to Scarlet.

Scarlet eased her chair back slowly.

The other mercenary pushed the hatch open, moving his rifle left, then right. He turned to Lanh. "Nothing."

Lanh looked at Scarlet, who shrugged. "Don't look at me. Jason bought this thing from an estate sale; the whole family was murdered on the boat while sailing to Panama. Gruesome stuff." She turned her head slightly, hoping Lanh wouldn't see the sweat beading on her forehead.

LET THERE BE LIGHT

"T̲h̲i̲s̲ ̲i̲s̲ ̲i̲t̲,̲ ̲c̲a̲p̲t̲a̲i̲n̲'̲s̲ ̲q̲u̲a̲r̲t̲e̲r̲s̲," A̲s̲a̲k̲o̲ ̲s̲a̲i̲d̲.

"You're sure?" Jason asked.

The Japanese woman pointed to a faded and worn plaque on the door. "Subtitles must be turned off."

Sofia looked at the small Japanese woman, then Jason. She pushed past her boss, whispering, "Burn."

The cabin was cramped by modern standards, barely enough room for Jason, Sofia, and Asako. Niles was forced to stand in the corridor to keep watch.

Jason whistled. "This is a goldmine." He pulled a book from a shelf, opening it and thumbing through the pages. He put the book back and looked around again. "Ama—"

Sofia put a hand over Jason's mouth. "I think we can retire that word for a little while." Jason nodded.

"His logbook," Asako whispered, pulling a large book from a safe in the bulkhead. "Whatever happened, the captain didn't have time to close his safe."

"What did happen here?" Sofia wondered. Her mind drifted back to the collection of corpses near the dock. Had they been trying to get aboard the sub? Who had welded the hatch open, ensuring the sub would never leave the bay?

Niles poked his head in the room. "While I'm not normally prone to claustrophobia, I must admit, I am not overly comfortable in these cramped quarters. I will keep watch from the boarding hatch." He squeezed his way down the corridor.

BACK IN THE MAIN COMPLEX SPACE, PHILLIPE BOUCHARD walked in. Another of his lieutenants, a Croatian man named Josip, walked over. "We've secured this room and I've sent men down the three tunnels we discovered." He hitched a thumb toward a single door. "Just past that security checkpoint." He pointed at another doorway, larger than the others in the space. "That way is the power plant. Tomas and Joe are working on it."

Bouchard nodded. "Good."

Josip continued, "One of the tunnels leads to barracks, the other a lab complex of some sort. The other two men haven't returned yet."

Bouchard grunted. "Send two more to check on the others. I want to have a rough idea of this place as soon as possible."

Without warning, hundred-year-old light bulbs glowed. Bouchard looked up. "It would seem your men got the power plant running. Let's go see." He headed toward the doorway Josip had initially indicated.

"TAKE THE LOGBOOK AND LET'S HEAD OUT," JASON URGED. "We've got hostiles to deal with. We can explore in depth once we figure out a solution to that well-armed problem." He turned and left the long dead captain's cabin.

From somewhere back the way they'd come, Niles' voice drifted in. "Jason, you should see this."

Jason picked up his pace, heading for the boarding hatch they'd come in through. When he arrived at the ladder, he looked up, seeing Nile's face looking over the lip of the hatch. The night vision goggles washed out as light poured in from somewhere. "The lights have come on." He looked at something beyond the submarine then back. "After a fashion."

Jason shooed him away from the hatch and climbed the ladder. When he cleared the outer hull of the ancient sub, he saw that dozens of lightbulbs had illuminated. He lifted his night vision goggles to his forehead, and after a brief moment of awe that lightbulbs from a hundred years ago still worked, he looked back down into the sub. "We gotta get going. Our mysterious pals figured out how to get the power on."

"Coming," Sofia said as Asako came into view, the log book tucked into a satchel the small woman had brought with her.

"I'm impressed any of these bulbs are still working but more impressed that the generator, or whatever this facility uses for power, is still functional," Niles commented as he offered a hand to Asako from the wooden deck.

Jason looked around the room, more impressed than he had been earlier now that the dim light of the ancient bulbs was bathing the room. He let out a low whistle.

He hopped from the sub back to the wooden dock. "We need to even the odds if we're going to keep this place from getting picked clean."

Jason nodded, looking at the door the two mercenaries tied up in the dockmaster's office had come through. "Yeah."

PART 4

TWELVE

MONSTER BOAT

"Who else is aboard this boat?" Lanh asked Scarlet.

The young redhead held up a finger. "One, your guys already searched the ship." Another finger. "Two, I told you, no one. Are you calling me a liar? That's rude, and not at all gentlemanly."

Lanh rubbed his face, then looked at his associate. "Go search the crew berths again."

The other man sighed loudly and exited the lounge. Lanh reached for a radio clipped to his belt. He held it up to his mouth. "Serge, status?"

A voice replied over the radio, "Nothing to report. The boss and the men made it to shore."

"Copy." Lanh lowered the radio, glaring at Scarlet. Before she could say or do anything, a scream came from somewhere deeper inside the *Raven*. Both of them spun to look at the open hatch.

"That doesn't sound good," Scarlet offered. She pushed the control on her chair to bring her toward the hatch.

Lanh stepped in front of her. "You stay here." He grabbed his radio. "Serge, get in here."

A minute later, a European man in his late thirties walked in.

"Keep an eye on her," Lanh ordered. When the other man nodded, Lanh went through the hatch deeper into the *Raven*.

"So, you're Serge? Neat name. Is it Peruvian?" Scarlet asked.

The man turned. "You talk a lot. Go to the corner and shut up." He pointed his submachine gun at her to emphasize his point.

Scarlet pushed the control on the arm of her chair back, guiding herself toward the indicated corner. Serge turned back toward the hatch his boss had gone through.

Scarlet slowly moved her hand down the side of her chair. She felt the shape of what she was looking for and removed it from the chair with a twist. She reached under her seat, feeling around until she found what she was looking for there, as well. That piece came loose with a slight jerk on it.

LANH TOOK THE STAIRS FROM THE MAIN DECK TO THE CREW berths. There was no sign of the man he'd just sent down there. "Henry?" he whispered. When he reached the first hatch, he nudged it open. Nothing. A room, a messy one, but nothing else; posters of marines and hot rods covered the walls, a partially disassembled pistol was on a soft cloth on the desk. The door opposite that one also held nothing but one of the crew's quarters, someone tidier.

A thunk sounded from further up the hallway. "Henry!" Lanh whispered, harsher this time. Lanh skipped the next four rooms, heading to where he'd thought the noise had come from. He took a deep breath and spun from the doorway to stand in the center of the open hatch, rifle aimed ahead of him. He came face to face with something from his nightmares, half flesh, half machine with glowing red eyes and flesh hanging from the exposed lower jaw bone. His finger twitched, firing a shot that hit the monster square in the chest. The bullet pinged off of a piece of metal barely hidden by what looked like rotting flesh, ricocheting back into the corridor. Before he could emit the scream that was on the tip of his tongue, the monster raised an arm and fired two needle sharp barbs. The moment the barbs struck the horrified mercenary, fifty thousand volts followed them, causing every muscle in Lanh's body to contract.

When the stunned mercenary hit the deck, Rufus grabbed his ankles and dragged him into the small storage room where Lanh's associate was propped against the back wall, also unconscious.

Rufus bent down, plucking radios from each man's belt. He then turned and exited the room, the magnetic lock engaging when the hatch closed.

The mechanical construct looked up and down the corridor, then headed for the elevator.

SCARLET REACHED FOR A THIRD COMPONENT, THIS ONE tucked in the arm of her chair, disguised as part of the control mechanism. Serge was still pacing the middle of the room, focused mostly on the hatch Lanh had gone through earlier. From the hallway Lanh had gone down, the elevator dinged.

Scarlet looked at Serge as he spun to look first down the hallway then back to his charge. She shrugged. When nothing further happened, Serge resumed his pacing until the elevator dinged once more. The mercenary spun and stomped over to Scarlet. "What the fuck is going on here?" he shouted at her. She recoiled as much as her chair would permit but still ended up with spittle on her face from the proximity of the frightened man.

"Dude, I don't know! I've been here with you!" She tried to keep her voice even, despite the muzzle of an automatic rifle being pointed at her midsection.

The elevator dinged again.

SO THAT'S WHY

Jason and the others were standing near the door they assumed led back to the main complex when they heard more voices from somewhere within the tunnel.

Jason looked at Sofia, who nodded, then to Niles and Asako, who scurried over to the same stack of crates they had hidden behind last time, just outside the dockmaster's office.

"You think those idiots are napping?" one voice said.

"Anything is possible with Max. That guy is so lazy, I don't know why the boss keeps hiring him." As the two mercenaries crossed the threshold, they fell silent as they saw the sub and the corpses all around it. Jason and Sofia jumped.

Taking care to not make the same mistake twice, Jason swung on his target quickly, making sure the butt of his pistol struck the man in the head cleanly. The mercenary grunted and stumbled forward. "The hell?" Jason muttered. Out of the corner of his eye, he saw Sofia fall upon her own target, putting the man in a choke hold and fighting against the much smaller man's struggles. Jason looked back just in time to avoid a jab from his own target. The roundhouse kick, however, he did not avoid, catching the mercenary's boot in his ribs. He caught the man's foot, and before the mercenary was able to shout, Jason lunged in with a swift and powerful kick to the man's crotch. The shout was choked off into a sad-sounding gurgle that ended in whimpering. Looking down at the man, Jason said, "Why are you assholes so hard to knock out?" He kicked the man in the face, rendering him very unconscious.

From behind him came a *thud* as Sofia released her man. She looked down at Jason's mercenary. "Better, though kind of low blow, the crotch kick." Jason shrugged.

They dragged the two men into the small office their other two captives were occupying, both now wide awake and wriggling and grunting.

Jason leaned down, removing the gag from the man he'd questioned before. "How many are you?"

The man looked at his two new roommates. "Two dozen if everyone is here. Boss was taking half the team over to your boat."

From behind Jason, Sofia groaned, "Ah, dios mio."

Jason sighed, pulled the gag back to the man's mouth, and stood. "We've got to get out of here and check on Scarlet." He produced more zip ties and secured the two new prisoners.

"Jason, that would have been hours ago. Whatever is happening or has happened on the *Raven* is already done," Niles said as he and Asako joined them. "Scarlet is smart and resourceful. Plus, when we left, she was secure in the Ops Center. There's enough ZapPow in the fridge to hold her over for days." The big South African man smiled at his friend. Jason nodded.

"Oh, my God," Asako said from the small desk she was standing next to, the captain's logbook laid out in front of her.

The others moved away from their prisoners. Niles asked, "What is it, Asako?" He moved to look over her shoulder as Jason and Sofia joined them.

Asako pointed to an entry, the last by the look of it. "They created a biological agent."

Jason looked around, standing up straight, making sure he was not touching the desk the logbook was resting on.

Asako shook her head. "I think the danger has passed. The captain mentioned that it has, had, a short lifespan outside a human body." She pointed to a section of writing. "He says he was scheduled to pick up the first batch and deliver it to the motherland."

"What happened?" Sofia asked.

"It doesn't say exactly." She moved her finger to what must have been the last part of the entry. "Here he mentions being told to weld the sub's hatch open by the base commander. The last thing he wrote was *I hope my wife knows I loved her.*" The small woman looked up at the others. "That's it."

Jason looked out the remains of the window at the sub and the corpses scattered around the dock. "Explains the bodies." He gestured toward the macabre pile. "Captain must be in the pile since he wasn't in his quarters."

"It does?" Niles asked, looking at his friend and employer.

Jason pointed to the sub. "Yeah, the general must have known that if the sub left, it could take the agent back to Japan. He came back to his boat, ordered his men to make the sub useless, and then went to his quarters to record this." He nodded to the logbook.

"I wonder where his body really is?" Niles said to no one in particular.

Asako shrugged. "That is a good question. I would expect—"

"Unless his body has the antidote, it's not important," Sofia interrupted. "You said it had a short lifespan?"

Asako gestured to the book. "The captain did, but yes."

Niles held up a hand. "I'm no biologist, but it is fairly safe to assume no virus or bacteria could survive in this environment for more than a few hours or days. Certainly not over one hundred years without a host to inhabit." He nodded toward the sub. "To be safe, don't swim in the bay, though."

Jason shuddered. "Okay, well gross, and good to know. So we're probably not infected and about to die?"

"Probably not," Niles replied.

DON'T MESS WITH REDHEADS

Serge approached the dinging elevator. From the lounge, Scarlet peered through the hatch, watching the unfolding action. The Croatian man was visibly shaking as he reached for the door. It would have been hard to not chuckle if she wasn't terrified herself, but for very different reasons...

As Serge's finger neared the call button, the doors to the small lift parted, revealing a darkened car with a metallic nightmare standing in the center. The red eyes shifted to make contact with Serge's. The Croatian man screamed as he stumbled back to avoid Rufus' reach. As bullets ricocheted off the metal framework of Rufus' ribs, it raised its other arm and fired two barbs into Serge's chest. He was unconscious before he finished falling.

Scarlet looked up at the camera pick up in the lounge's corner. "Good job, girl! How many are left?"

From the nearest speaker, the *Raven's* AI whispered, "There is just one left, and he is on his way. I assume he heard the gunshots. I apologize for not disabling this man before he could fire his weapon. Would you like me to have Rufus intercept him?"

Scarlet shook her head once. "No, he can't move that fast. He wouldn't have the element of surprise. I'll deal with the last one."

"Please be careful," the AI said. Rufus reached down and picked up the unconscious mercenary. "I will secure this one with the other two." Rufus headed back into the elevator, dragging Serge.

Scarlet rolled back to the lounge and toward the large glass doors at the front of the large room that opened to the forward deck of the boat, where luxurious outdoor couches and chairs were arrayed. In her lap was the stunner she'd assembled from the various parts she kept hidden in her chair.

It took only a few seconds for the last mercenary to round the corner of the superstructure on the port side. "Hey! What are you doing out here?" he asked, his thick Croatian accent giving away his country of origin. "Where is Serge? You are supposed to stay inside." He gestured toward the large open doors and the lounge beyond. "Go back inside." He used his machine gun to point.

Scarlet rolled backward a bit. "Okay, okay, it's just that... well... Serge needs your help, that's it. He's in trouble."

His gun was held at the ready, not aimed at Scarlet but ready to fire should he need to. "What do you mean, trouble?" She pointed toward the hatch inside the lounge that lead deeper into the ship. The man pulled his radio from his belt. "Serge? Lanh? Come in?" As he turned slightly to look into the lounge, Scarlet raised her homemade pistol and fired. Unlike a traditional taser, the stunner she had built was a custom design of her own creation. It fired a high energy pulse of sound that short-circuited the target's central nervous system briefly. The mercenary didn't even register what happened as his limbs stopped functioning and he collapsed to the ground unconscious.

"Clean up, aisle three," she said, loud enough for Oracle to hear. The stunner dropped back into her lap as she ran both hands through her hair. She exhaled loudly.

"ARE YOU SURE THIS IS A GOOD IDEA?" NILES ASKED, huffing from rolling a drum of diesel from one corner of the sub bay to the dock.

"We need to lure as many of the bad guys as we can here, so we can, I hope, block them in. The only way this base isn't pillaged is if we keep control of it." He jerked his head toward Asako, perched on a crate, the logbook of the deceased captain in her lap. "Whatever killed these folks is here somewhere in a test tube or fridge or something." He shook his head. "Too risky."

The heavyset man nodded. "Fair point." He rapped his knuckles on the drum. "This is the last."

Jason nodded and made a low whistle. Sofia poked her head out of the sub's hatch. "This is the last," he said. She nodded and dropped back inside the sub.

Jason turned to Niles. "You and Asako should get going. Remember, don't leave the tunnel. Wait for us at the end."

Niles grunted as he picked up his satchel and headed for his friend, still intently reading the logbook they'd found.

Jason hopped up onto the sub, careful not to disturb the wire running from inside the sub to a small package taped to the nearest drum of fuel.

THIRTEEN

BOOM

THE EXPLOSION IN THE SUB BAY ROCKED THE ENTIRE
complex, dislodging a century's worth of dust from every nook
and cranny. Phillipe Bouchard and his men all crouched as
debris and dust rained down. The lights that had only recently
come on dimmed slightly, some flickering and burning out.
When the shaking stopped, the French treasure hunter looked
at his men, pointing to the doorway that led to the three tunnels
making up the rest of the facility. "Go find out what happened."

Most of the men standing around him hurried off through
the ancient security checkpoint. From where Bouchard was
standing, he couldn't tell where the smoke he could see was
coming from.

One of his men leaned out of the doorway. "Boss, it's
coming from door three."

Because none of the doors beyond the security checkpoint
had labels, the men had referred to them by numbers.

Bouchard waved dismissively. "I don't care. Go." The man
ducked back into the small chamber of tunnels.

Bouchard looked at the two men who remained with him.

"Stay sharp. I'd put money on that explosion being related to Jason Kincaid and his team, whom you've still not located."

The nearest man bowed. "Sorry, Boss, we've looked all over." Bouchard headed for the old security checkpoint his men had gone through. One of the men raised a hand. "Uh, Boss, where are you going?"

"The lab, see what I can find."

JASON AND SOFIA STUMBLED INTO THE OPENING OF THE tunnel they had entered the sub bay through, both coughing profusely.

Sofia doubled over. "That seemed," a cough, "like a great idea," another cough, "on paper."

Jason patted the ex-marine on the back between his own coughs. "Yeah, we probably should have been in the tunnel before blowing the charges." He looked back into the bay at the smoking ruin of the dock and the now nearly sunk submarine. Flames still clung to the metal of the vessel where diesel fuel hadn't burned off completely.

Sofia straightened, nodding to Jason. "Come on." He nodded.

It took far less time to traverse the tunnel back to the main complex than it had earlier. Niles and Asako were hunched together just inside the secret door back into the base general's office. The two jumped slightly as Jason and Sofia approached them. Niles looked the two of them up and down. "That sounded louder than expected."

"There may or may not have been more diesel used than needed," Jason said as he pushed past the two academics, easing up the floor tile that hid the entrance to the secret tunnel just enough to peek into the room. He looked down at the group and nodded, whispering, "Clear."

He slid the floor panel over as quietly as possible, aware that the door to the admin office was now wide open. As Niles came up out of the hole, he slammed his knee against the inner edge of the entrance to the secret tunnel. His grunt made Jason wince.

From inside the tunnel, Sofia's harsh whisper came. "Are you trying to get us found?"

The heavyset man groaned, "What? It hurt."

From below him Sofia whispered, "We'll work on your new fitness routine when we get home."

Jason crept through the outer office into the hallway. He looked around. The other office doors were all open, the offices now moderately well lit, thanks to whatever the other team had done to the power plant for the old base. He peeked out the door that led into the main complex. Two men were standing around the desks looking through the left-behind detritus scattered here and there. One was looking through the sole drawer in the desk on the right.

He returned to the others gathered in the general's outer office. "Just two," he whispered.

Sofia nodded and moved to join Jason. She turned to Niles and Asako. "Wait—"

"—here. Yes, we know the drill," Asako replied.

"Our guests are secure, Scarlet," Oracle said from the speaker in the ceiling of the Ops Center, back at her normal volume.

After the last mercenary had been incapacitated and locked in the storage room by Scarlet and her homemade stunner, Scarlet had gone around the lounge and lower level, collecting the dropped weapons and taking them all to the Ops Center. A few ZapPows later, and the team's hacker was back in her technological cocoon in the Ops Center, surrounded by displays. She looked at the ceiling. "Good job. Have we received any comms from the team?"

"One moment," the ceiling speaker replied. A moment later the AI continued, "Sorry, controlling Rufus took a significant amount of my processing power. I was unable to monitor ship's systems during my adventure saving you. No, we received no comms signals from the away team."

"No apology needed. You kicked ass at the saving me thing." She rubbed her chin as she tapped absently on the desk at her side. "What are you doing over there, Jason?" She looked at the display showing Emmet's status. "Damn, Emmet's gonna need a recharge soon. When he hits fifteen percent, go ahead and bring him in, in case I'm not paying attention."

"Acknowledged. Should we move the *Raven* closer to where the team went ashore?" Oracle asked.

"No, let's stay here and keep an eye on things." She looked at the monitor showing the boat Phillipe Bouchard had arrived on. "If we move, they'll move. Let's monitor our pal Phillipe's boat, see what's up over there. See if you can figure out how many baddies are over there."

"Acknowledged."

Scarlet set about working her various keyboards and track-pads, humming to herself as she did.

One deck below the Ops Center where the crew berths were located, several *thuds* were coming from a storage room near the elevator. Inside the small space, four mercenaries were awake and wiggling around on the floor, their arms and legs bound, which didn't stop them from trying to kick the door. Outside the door, Rufus stood guard.

JASON AND SOFIA CREPT TOWARD THE TWO MERCENARIES, still hanging around the vacated work desks at the front of the main complex.

Jason looked at Scarlet, nodded. He bent down and picked up a piece of, well, something— he wasn't sure what—and tossed it. When it hit a desk, one of the men spun to look toward the noise. Unfortunately, the other spun to look for the cause of the noise. His eyes locked on Jason's. "Who?" the startled mercenary said as Jason dashed toward him.

Sofia, seeing that her window was about to close, removed something from the thigh pocket on her pants. She hurled the object at her target as he turned to look at his comrade. His head jerked back as a piece of C4 hit him squarely in the face. Before the stunned man could react, she tackled him to the ground. Sofia wasted no time putting the man in a sleeper hold until his thrashing stopped.

Jason and his mercenary were also on the ground rolling around, but the hired gun was not going down as easily. While Jason had managed to knock the automatic rifle from the man's grip, he had lost one of his pistols in the scuffle. His remaining pistol was still secured in its holster. Sofia shook her head. "Idiot." She stood and watched as the two men traded blows as they rolled around on the floor. They collided with one of the centuries-old desks, knocking it over. Sofia groaned, looking at the contents of the desk as Jason and mercenary rolled over them. "Those were probably worth something." She looked around, realizing that Jason and his new friend might attract attention with the destruction of the desk.

Jason got the upper hand and landed a solid cross, knocking the mercenary out. He stood up, panting, "Fuck, why do I always get the hard ones?"

Sofia tutted, "You just aren't very good." He raised his middle finger. "You're very good at other things," she offered as a consolation.

Niles and Asako came out of hiding, each now having a large and very old rucksack on their shoulders.

Jason motioned to the large bags. "Going on a trip?"

Asako made a face. "At the pace you're destroying things, Niles and I decided to try to save what we can carry." She tilted her head to her shoulder. "We found these in that office."

Jason glanced over to the unconscious mercenary and the debris on the surrounding floor from the overturned desk. He looked back. "That's probably not a bad idea."

THE ROOM THAT HELD THE BASE POWER PLANT WAS CLOSER to a rough-hewn cave than a room. A diesel electric motor sat in the middle of the space surrounded by a dozen centuries' old fuel drums and hastily abandoned toolboxes. Despite its age, it had only taken the mercenaries an hour to clean up the machine and get it running again, restoring power to the entire subterranean facility.

Unbeknownst to Phillipe and his mercenaries, the ancient power plant also powered an analog timing device that, until then, had been sitting dormant. With power restored, its countdown resumed.

ANOTHER EXPLOSION RUMBLED THROUGH THE BASE, shaking more dust loose and freeing small avalanches of pebbles here and there. Phillipe Bouchard looked around the laboratory he was in. "Que se passe-t-il?" Several of the strings of lights strung from the rock ceiling were swaying slightly. One of the worktables near the door to the laboratory space spilled several glass tubes and vials to the floor, shattering them.

He turned to head back to the opening that led down the tunnel back to the main complex when he heard voices. Voices that didn't belong to any of his men. He spun twice, taking in the room. Few places to hide. His eyes settled on a tall cabinet in the corner of the room, opposite the doorway. He sprinted for it.

"I'm just saying that we have to figure out our next steps. That little cave-in won't stop those goons from digging out, especially once they see all those bodies," Sofia argued.

Jason answered, "Don't forget their friends in the office. Once they find them, they'll know they're not alone down here."

The group entered the lab section of the base. Niles and Asako both rushed in, touching everything they could.

Sofia watched, then said, "Do you think touching everything you see is wise?" The two academics immediately stopped and moved their hands to their sides. The small Asian woman turned, bowed slightly, and continued on into the room.

Jason turned to his colleague. "Yeah, knowing we're here and being spooked by a pile of bodies will be a good motivator. I'm thinking we head back out, make contact with the *Raven* and Scarlet, and call in the authorities. We've seen enough and established our find, so it shouldn't be hard to defend our claim on this place."

"Uh, Jason?" Niles said from across the room.

Jason continued, not hearing his friend, "Plus we can probably keep whoever these guys are holed up inside until someone with more firepower arrives."

"Jason!"

Jason and Sofia turned to see Niles, his hands up in the air, facing a man in a fedora holding a submachine gun to Asako's temple.

"Oh." It was all Jason could think to say.

"Hello, Monsieur Kincaid, it is a pleasure to meet you," the mystery man said, smiling.

Sofia shifted her grip on her rifle, only to have the mystery man tut and nod to her.

"No, no, mon cher. Please put your gun," he turned to nod to Jason, "and yours on the table over there and then return to where you are." He looked at Niles. "Please, sir, join your friends over there."

Niles glared but offered no resistance to the idea, slowly walking toward Jason and Sofia.

"So, you've managed to take out all of my men? That is truly impressive," the man said, never letting his grip on Asako or his gun loosen. "I must say I am in awe. Your reputation appears well deserved."

Jason inclined his head, his eyes never leaving those of the other man. "They're alive, probably, I think. But yeah, it's just you and however many didn't head to the sub bay. Why don't you let her go and we can let you be on your way? You don't have to be here when the authorities arrive."

The man tutted again, "Alas, no. That is not an option at all. Those men out there, while obviously not as good as I was led to believe, were not cheap. The only way to not—how do you Americans say it—*lose my shirt,* is to deliver this base to my employer, receive my handsome payment, and be on my way." He smiled, but his eyes remained deadly serious. "I have a counterproposal. You and your people leave. I can call ahead to have my men leave your vessel." He nudged his weapon against Asako's temple. "I will, of course, have to hold on to her until I am sure you are out of my hair."

"No deal," Sofia growled before Jason could say anything. He looked over to her. She didn't look at him, her eyes never leaving the mystery man in the fedora.

Jason looked at the man. "By the way, who the hell are

you?"

FOURTEEN

STORM'S A COMIN'

THE FEDORA-WEARING MAN BOWED AS MUCH AS HE COULD with Asako in his grip. "My name is Phillipe Bouchard."

Jason grunted, "I've heard of you, treasure hunter for hire." He hitched a thumb in the general direction of the sub bay. "Uses mercenaries to do his dirty work, which is at least rumored to include murder."

"Such an ugly word, but I won't lie. I am paid well to do my job, and that includes removing impediments. I do my job well. I am sure, as a professional yourself, you can appreciate that."

Sofia grunted.

Bouchard nodded toward the door Jason and the others had just come through. "Why don't we retire to the main complex? You can help free my men from whatever it is you did to them. You mentioned *piles of bodies?*"

Asako took a deep breath, trying not to move too much. "We discovered what this base was for and what happened to the base personnel."

The Frenchman glanced down at his prisoner. "Do tell."

Jason raised a hand, cutting off the Asian woman's impending story. "We collapsed the tunnel to the submarine bay. Your guys might dig their way out, I don't know, but there's a tunnel that connects the general's office to the bay. We'll show you. Your guys can get out that way." He hung his head.

"See, not so hard," Bouchard said, smiling again. He motioned with his gun briefly toward the doorway. "Let us go."

"Well, that's no good," Scarlet uttered as she rubbed her face. She looked from one monitor to another. "Oracle, how up to date is your weather data?"

"I have a solid data link, laggy as it is, with several satellites. It is updated every minute."

Scarlet pulled up a menu on the main computer of her technology nest. "Afraid of that." She tapped a few keys. The screen to her right updated, showing a weather map, Graham Island in the center. The storm they'd traveled through last night had moved on toward the mainland, but another was moving in from the ocean and looked like it was going to travel right over the top of the island and the inlet the *Raven* was floating in. As if waiting for just the right moment, a gust of wind slammed into the *Raven*.

"I advise we drop the anchor," Oracle offered from the ceiling speaker.

Scarlet pressed the button that released her from her workstation. She looked up. "Do it." She rolled out of the Ops Center as the entire boat tilted slightly as another gust struck the *Raven*. "Better turn us into the wind, too," she said.

"Ack— Scarlet, I do not have access to the engines or our maneuvering system."

Scarlet stopped. "What do you mean? I gave you full access."

"It appears someone has tampered with the engines."

Scarlet slammed her hand on the control stick for her chair, changing her direction in the hallway. As the elevator doors opened and she punched the down arrow, she asked, "How is that possible?"

"I am afraid I do not know. I am reviewing log files now."

Scarlet sighed and put her hands out to the sides of the small lift as the *Raven* rocked again. "Damn, this storm is moving fast."

"It is indeed," Oracle agreed.

The elevator doors parted and Scarlet rolled into a hallway that was much more utilitarian than the one above. Conduits and bundles of wire ran the length of the hallway in the upper corners. Normally, the below-decks space was kept tidy, and rarely visited, since Scarlet and Jason were the only two members of the team who knew how to work on the guts of their home away from home. "Well, someone has been down here mucking around," Scarlet mumbled to herself. Several wire trunks were dangling from ceiling brackets, cut. A pool of liquid had formed near the door leading to the main engineering space. When Scarlet rolled to the door, it opened automatically, revealing the mess that was now the engineering space. The boat lurched as another wind gust slammed into it. "This is not good."

WHAT'S A LITTLE ENGINE REPAIR BETWEEN FRIENDS?

"Scarlet, we are drifting closer to the shore of the island," Oracle said from the speaker in the corner of the ceiling of the engineering compartment.

"Great, thanks. No pressure." She grumbled as she pushed a piece of engine cowling to the side, allowing her to roll closer. Looking around she spotted several severed wire bundles. "That croissant-eating bastard." She looked at the speaker in the ceiling. "You figure out what happened? How did they get down here without you knowing?" She pulled a bundle of wires out as far as they would go and began stripping the insulation.

"I believe I have," the AI answered. "I found several checksum discrepancies in my log files. I believe someone came down to this level, caused the damage you are attempting to fix, and then went next door and deleted log files." A pause as the AI thought about it. "I do not know how they gained access to those logs. I would say someone on Mr. Bouchard's payroll is an expert in computers."

Scarlet started splicing the stripped wires back into the other end of the damaged bundle. She huffed, "Makes sense. Wonder which one of them is the smart one?"

The boat rocked. "I cannot say. I can say that we are now even closer to the shore of the island."

"Thanks for that." Scarlet finished splicing a wire together. "Are you keeping tracking of the data busses? Are we making progress?"

"I am and we are. There are only five connections left to re-establish my connection to the engines."

Scarlet grabbed another wire. "Okay, give me a minute." She worked quickly splicing wires, swearing when accidentally touching one that had current running through it, and groaning when a piece would break, requiring more splicing.

"I have a connection," Oracle said as Scarlet released the last wire, shoving the bundle back into place as best she could. "I have bad news, Scarlet." The *Raven* rocked again.

Scarlet drummed her fingers on the arm of her chair. "Of course you do. What's up?"

"The engine is reporting several faults, as are the maneuvering thrusters."

Scarlet looked around. "Am I wrong in that we need maneuvering more right now?"

"You are not. Our current situation would be most quickly solved by repairing the maneuvering thrusters," the AI replied.

Scarlet adjusted herself in her seat, then guided her chair over to a large device in the opposite corner of the engineering space from the main motor and generator. "Oh, I see. Damn, they really did a number down here." She looked up. "Make a note to add some additional security layers to this room in the future."

"Noted."

Using a small powered screwdriver, Scarlet removed a panel on the side of the pump that drove the maneuvering thrusters. "If we find out which bozo did this, I want you to have Rufus throttle him."

"I cannot cause harm to humans," the AI replied matter-of-factly.

"What about a thorough shake?"

"I could do that."

Scarlet reached inside the pump, feeling around. With her free hand, she grabbed a flashlight from a pouch on the arm of her chair, shining it inside the cavity. Something inside made a loud click sound. "Yes!" Scarlet withdrew her hand. She looked at the ceiling. "Anything?"

The machine Scarlet just had her hand in made a series of *cthunk* sounds, then began to rumble in a constant pattern. Assuming that to be a good sign, Scarlet reached down and grabbed the cover she had removed and began re-attaching it. From overhead, Oracle confirmed her assumption. "Yes, I have maneuvering control and the thrusters are working. I have added an entry in your to-do list to run a full diagnostic on them, but they will keep us from being dashed against the rocks of the island."

"Colorful."

"We were close to crashing on the rocks," the AI replied tartly.

"How close?"

"You do not want to know."

Scarlet grunted. "Okay, time to get the engine up and running." She reached down and pressed a button on the arm of her chair, and a small panel slid open, revealing a two small buttons. She pressed the green one. Her chair clicked and whirred.

After discovering their missing colleagues in the dockmaster's office, the mercenaries, as a group, went back to the collapsed entrance. They formed a bucket brigade-style line from the rubble as far down the corridor as possible toward the sub bay, moving rocks of all sizes away from the collapse that had trapped them.

While they were busy trying to free themselves, no one noticed that the water level of the harbor, where the severely damaged sub was resting, was rising.

ALTERNATE ROUTE ADVISED

Loud shouts came from the entry to the tunnel
that led to the sub bay as Jason, Sofia, and Niles exited into the
security corridor with doorways to all the ancillary sections of
the ancient base. Bouchard and Asako followed. The doorway
leading to the sub bay was collapsed, but gaps near the top
showed flashlight beams and allowed angry voices to get
through.

"They sound mad," Sofia deadpanned.

Bouchard nodded. "You trapped them." He turned toward
the single door that led to the main complex. "Come, show me
this tunnel." He gestured the others to lead.

As they made their way across the main complex space,
Asako looked up at her captor. "What do you want with this
place?"

The Frenchman gestured with his free hand for Niles to
move further from him, having seen him drift closer and closer,
perhaps to attempt a rescue. He said, "I want nothing of this
place. My employer, however, will probably want every single
thing here. I suspect even the letterhead will fetch a tremendous
price on the collector's market." He grinned. "Not to mention

214

the museums who will undoubtedly clamor for access. My cut should be quite handsome."

From ahead, Jason asked, "And who is your employer? How'd they know about this base?"

"Ah yes, I have told this story to your lovely handicapped associate—" Bouchard said but had to stop to point his gun at Jason, who had stopped walking and turned to face the Frenchman. "Tsk, tsk, Mr. Kincaid, keep moving." He tilted his head. "I assure you your employee is quite all right. I left some of my men aboard your wonderful boat to keep an eye on her. She will be fine, as will you, so long as you cause me no further trouble."

The general's office was much like Jason and the others had left it. He moved to the floor panel and slid it aside. "There's a similar panel in the sub bay."

Bouchard looked at Jason and was about to say something when the sound of stone grinding on stone echoed throughout the base, followed by a low-level rumble that shook more dust loose.

Bouchard motioned for Jason to enter the tunnel. "Best hurry. We'll be here waiting." He gestured for one of his men who had met them in the main complex to accompany Jason. Jason scowled, then descended the stairs into the tunnel, an armed mercenary right behind him, rifle at the ready.

"That shaking is new," Niles observed. "This island can't be geologically unstable." He tapped his chin in thought and focused on the tremors, forgetting the armed man standing nearby.

Asako looked from Niles to Sofia, hoping the latter might reveal some type of plan with just her eyes. Instead, the tall Hispanic woman simply raised an eyebrow in question when Asako made eye contact. The petite Asian woman sighed.

IT DIDN'T TAKE LONG TO RETRACE THE ROUTE THROUGH the secret tunnel to the sub bay. Jason slid the floor panel aside and left the tunnel, followed by his guard. The mercenary motioned for Jason to move to the nearby wall while he leaned into the opening of the main access tunnel and shouted for his comrades.

Jason looked over to the ruined sub and noticed the water level was considerably higher than before. "What the..." he said to himself as he squinted in the low light to take in the artificial harbor. The water was definitely higher, nearly spilling-over-the-wall higher.

The mercenary returned, followed by the sound of several people returning down the tunnel. When the first man emerged, covered in dust and dirt, he glared at Jason. Jason blushed and smiled, figuring bravado wasn't called for in this situation. When everyone was gathered, the initial mercenary that accompanied Jason told one of the others to head down the tunnel, then pointed to Jason to follow. The rest of the mercenaries followed him into the tunnel, no one bothering to reseat the floor panel that had hidden the tunnel.

BAD GUYS AT FULL STRENGTH

THE WAIT WASN'T LONG. ONE OF THE TRAPPED mercenaries came out of the tunnel, followed by Jason and the first mercenary barely ten minutes later. The rest of the trapped mercenaries followed them out of the tunnel, crowding the general's office.

As the large group crowded into the not-that-large general's office, the base shook again, the sound of grinding stone came from somewhere distant. Bouchard pointed to one of his men. "Their weapons are in the lab space. Go get them." The man nodded and dashed away as the rest of the group filed out into the office and hallway beyond the general's office.

As the group left the small office bloc, another tremor rumbled through the base. Bouchard pointed to another man. "Go find out what's happening." He gestured to the rest of his men. "Take those two to the barracks and guard them. I have need of these two." Four of the remaining mercenaries nodded and shoved Jason and Sofia toward the doorway to the security corridor and a door they hadn't gone through yet, the last of the three in the small security area. Bouchard turned to the two remaining members of the group from the *Raven*. "I believe you can be useful."

Niles, though, deep in thought, mumbled, "These tremors seem to be fairly regularly occurring. Interesting."

Bouchard gestured to the door leading back to the main base facility. "Come, let us move to less cramped quarters." When Niles didn't immediately move Bouchard jabbed him with his pistol.

With his men back, Bouchard pushed Asako to join Niles as the group headed out of the office bloc.

Niles looked at their captor. "You were explaining who your boss was?" Hopefully, the seemingly chatty Frenchman would continue. Niles hoped that would buy more time for Jason and Sofia, mostly Sofia, to do something amazing and get the upper hand.

"As I told your friend on the boat, my employer is a wealthy biotech something or other. He explained his pedigree to me, but I didn't care. He has apparently hacked into several universities in order to gather intel and potentially poach or hijack discoveries, particularly those in the biotech sector.

"My understanding is that a professor in Vancouver emailed a colleague regarding the ridiculous theory a friend of theirs was sharing around campus. This professor had an extraordinarily low regard for the rumor, outside of laughing at it. His email to a colleague in his department was scanned by my employer, who took an interest. While outside his primary area of interest, he recognized the value on the collector's market for World War Two memorabilia from an until-now unknown secret Japanese base." The Frenchman smiled. "The stuff of thriller novels, oui?"

Niles tutted, "Indeed."

Asako blushed. "Who was it that sent the email?"

"Excuse me?" Bouchard replied.

"The email. The one making fun of the idea of this base," she pressed.

Bouchard snapped his fingers. "I see." He bowed. "Please do not take offense, ma chérie. You have, after all, been vindicated."

The small woman fumed. "Small consolation, being mocked behind my back!" She stomped a foot. The room trembled, and the sound of stone grinding against stone echoed through the space.

Bouchard raised an eyebrow. "Small but mighty." He chuckled at his joke, no one else did. He turned serious faster than Niles could process, "Which reminds me," He aimed his pistol at Asako and fired.

"Are you mad?" Niles shrieked as he rushed to Asako's side. She was on the ground, moaning. Niles looked her over, finding the would, her shoulder. He looked up at the Frenchman, "Why in God's name did you shoot her?"

Bouchard smiled his frighteningly not friendly smile, "To ensure I had your attention and that you knew I was serious." He nodded to Asako, "It is but a flesh wound." He turned and walked away.

"Asshole." Asako ground out through clenched teeth.

FIFTEEN

BEDTIME

The barracks space was about half as big as the main lab complex structure. The bulk of the room was metal bunk beds, with a few doors on one side, presumably the restroom and showers. More of the pre-fab office wall pieces lined one side of the space, forming semiprivate sleeping quarters.

Looking at the pre-fab space, Sofia mumbled, "Officer country."

Jason looked at her, then headed toward a section of the bunks, most still with their sheets and blankets on them, dusty as they may have been. Small trunks were stored under each. He turned to their guards. "This is cool. Have you all been in here before? Any museum around would pay a mint for this stuff."

The guards exchanged glances. The tallest, an African man, said, "Don't wander off. Boss said to keep you here. He didn't say we couldn't tie you to a bed. Don't make us."

A gunshot echoed through the base, the stone causing it to sound as loud as if it was in the same room. Jason and Sophia looked at each other, sharing a worried expression.

Sofia turned to the guard, made a show of looking the man

up and down, "You can tie me to anything you like, papi." She winked. The mercenary nearest the man smacked him in the chest. "You need us to give you some privacy?" He made a suggestive gesture and indicated the barely private officer's sleeping area.

The man blushed a shade darker. "Nah, man. Boss would have a fit, plus she's not my type." His eyes drifted over to Jason, who turned to inspect a foot locker, blushing.

Sofia turned slowly to pretend to look at one of the bunks, personal effects still taped to it and tucked into the top bunk mattress. "Didn't see that coming," she mumbled to herself as she pulled a yellowing photo out from under the mattress springs. It showed a young Japanese couple, the man in uniform. She slid the picture into a pocket on her shirt.

Jason made it to the far side of the room, the tall African guard and one other trailing him warily. He pointed to a propaganda poster stuck to the wall outside one of the officer's quarters. "This is fantastic." He looked at the taller guard, trying his best to smile invitingly, or what he assumed was an inviting smile. "There are entire exhibits dedicated to Japanese war propaganda, and most of what I've seen in this base isn't on display anywhere. It's all new. This place is a treasure trove." He beamed.

The shorter guard perked up. "Treasure?" He looked around, then shoved Jason out of the way to look inside the officer's sleeping space. Unlike his companion this guard was of Asian descent and not well muscled.

From the opposite side of the room one of the other mercenaries shouted, "Holy shit, what the hell is that?"

Jason and his guards trotted over to join Sofia and her guards. Three bodies were lying near the wall, swords run through their desiccated, but otherwise largely intact, bodies.

"Seppuku," Jason muttered. He made a show of kneeling

down to examine the bodies while staying clear of the swords. He turned to look at the guards, all standing together. "They killed themselves."

The tall guard nodded. "We—" He looked around. "I know what Seppuku means." He smiled down at Jason. Was that a twinkle in his eye? He turned to the other guards, "Ritual suicide."

The other three guards exchanged glances. "Why'd they kill themselves?" one asked. A short Arab man.

Jason grinned. "In Japanese culture, when one has brought great shame to themselves, they can commit Seppuku as a way to restore honor to one's family." He made a slashing motion across his belly.

Sofia had moved to be behind and between two of the guards, dwarfing both of them. She nodded to Jason. When he finished making his slashing motion, he pantomimed his guts spilling out on to the floor. The guards, all but the African, reared back in disgust. Sofia made her move. She grabbed each of the guards in front of her by the head and slammed them together. The crack was disturbingly loud. Jason winced, as did the other two guards.

Jason took that moment to grab the no-longer-needed tantō knife from one of the bodies and lunged toward the guard next to the African man, a much smaller target. "Sorry!" he shouted as he plunged the knife into the man's shoulder. He followed the stab with an elbow to the face, knocking the mercenary out cold.

Jason moved as fast as he could, knowing he was within arm's reach of the largest of the four guards. He was too slow, a muscular black skinned hand grabbed his shoulder like a vice grip.

BIG GUNS

Scarlet's chair shifted under her. A metal band unfolded and enclosed her waist as the chair began to move, raising her body. The two larger wheels slid further apart as two struts formed around her withered legs. The powered rear wheels moved into position near her feet, forming high tech rollerblades.

"I did not know your chair could do that?" Oracle said from the overhead speaker as the now standing and wheeled Scarlet rolled over to the main engine. Despite the maneuvering thrusters being operational, the wind and growing swells in the inlet were fighting to toss the *Raven* this way and that—an excellent test of the gyroscopic stabilizers in the upright mode of Scarlet's wheelchair.

Scarlet grinned. "I do have my secrets, you know." She shrugged. "I never thought I'd need to use it, but here we are." She leaned over the engine to inspect the damage. As she leaned, she wobbled slightly. "Gonna take some getting used to, haven't rollerbladed in a while."

"If you connect the main data trunk, the blue wire, back into the main data board to your left, I should be able to run a diagnostic on the engine," Oracle said. As Scarlet rooted around in the engine housing looking for the blue data cable, Oracle asked, "Will you remain in this more mobile configuration from now on?"

Scarlet brushed at the connector then plugged the wire into the data port in the engine control board. "That do it?"

A few seconds passed. "It did," Oracle confirmed. "I am starting the diagnostic. It should only take a minute."

"Cool. And to answer your question, no. Once we've got the *Raven* back up and running, I'm disengaging this." She gestured to her legs, bound into in the upright frame supporting her, balanced on the two primary wheels of her chair. "Isn't me."

"I do not understand. Do you not want to be more like you used to be? Like the others?" the AI asked.

"No. This is me now. I'm not going to pretend otherwise."

"I see."

"You don't, but that's okay. It's a human thing," Scarlet replied, smiling at the ceiling.

"I have completed the diagnostic. There is good news and bad news."

Scarlet picked up a wrench. "Of course. Hit me. Bad, then good. Let's end on a high note."

"Very well, the bad news is that the other vessel is moving closer. The good news is that you only need to reset the control board to its factory settings. I can then flash the memory module with the last back up I have stored. That will restore functionality."

"What's the other boat doing?" Scarlet asked as she worked the housing of the control board of the engine loose.

"It is coming toward us; I have counted five men aboard. Four are on the bow, and they are armed. One is in the bridge." After a pause, "There, now if you could just press the yellow button and the blue down at the same time, careful not to unplug it from the engine." When Scarlet pressed the buttons, Oracle said, "Hold for fifteen seconds." After fifteen seconds passed, "Release."

Scarlet followed the directions and when the lights on the control panel flashed three times, she set about re-attaching it to the engine. "How long?"

"Five minutes," Oracle replied.

"You can keep us off the rocks with the thrusters, right?"

"Correct, but that is about it. The thrusters are not powerful enough for more, given the current conditions," the AI offered.

Scarlet rolled out of the engine room, toward the elevator and the Ops Center above. As she did, she reached down and pressed a recessed button near her thigh. As she rolled, her standing frame shifted back into a wheelchair, slowly lowering her and adjusting her body to a sitting position.

RISING WATER

THE LARGE MAN PULLED JASON BY THE SHOULDER INTO A bear hug, thrashing back and forth, shaking Jason like a dog's toy.

Sofia, now armed with the rifle one of her guards had been holding, was aiming it at Jason and the large guard. "No shot," she said cooly.

As the man thrashed back and forth, he moved away from Sofia. Jason waited until the thrashing brought him in line with one of the bunk beds. He brought his legs up and pushed as hard as he could against the old bed. The bed toppled, but so did the guard. His grip on Jason loosened enough for the much smaller man to force an elbow into the large guard's midsection. As the guard wheezed, Jason scrambled away from him on all fours, almost. A vise-like grip latched onto his ankle, causing him to scream.

"Did you just scream?" Sofia asked, standing several feet away, still tracking the melee with her rifle. She looked at the guard. "Please stop. You're far too cute to put a bullet in, even if you play for the other team."

The guard looked up at the ex-marine and released Jason.

He growled as he and Jason stood at the same time. Jason looked at the man as he moved to stand closer to his companion. "It wasn't a scream."

"Uh huh, sure." She smirked.

"It sounded like a scream," the other man offered.

Jason looked at the man. "One, shut up. Two, no offense—you are intensely handsome. It's just I don't get involved with mercenaries. You seem smart. I'm sure you could find other work. Better work." The man bared his teeth and shrugged.

Sofia handed Jason a pistol from one of the guards and knelt to rummage through the myriad pockets and pouches in their uniforms. She withdrew zip ties and moved to take care of the three unconscious men. Looking at the one with the knife wound, she looked at Jason. "Savage."

He shrugged. "I said I was sorry."

Thinking he had an opportunity, the African man took a step toward Jason, who immediately re-aimed his pistol center mass on the man. "Cute, not stupid," he said, smiling. The other man scowled.

Sofia walked over and gestured for the man to put his hands behind his back. As she secured him with two zip ties, she leaned toward his ear. "Coulda been so much fun," she tutted.

Jason shook his head as he watched her. "So inappropriate." He leaned down and hefted one of the smaller guards up over his shoulder. "Let's put 'em in one of the far rooms." He nodded toward one of the doors set in the wall opposite the doorway that led back to the main complex. As he headed toward the indicated door, the floor shook again.

Once they'd secured the guards to each other, back to back, they headed for the doorway back to the main complex.

"We're still very outnumbered," Sofia observed, checking her rifle.

Jason grunted. "Well, yeah, but, you know...we have you." He smiled. "Do we know how many are left?"

Sofia shook her head.

IN THE NOW-EMPTY SUB BAY, THE WATER HAD RISEN WELL above the concrete berm that formed the artificial bay. The ravaged sub was nearly submerged, and water was approaching the dockmaster's office. The sound of stone grinding against stone rumbled through the base, something made a sound like a dry twig snapping and the water level surged, rushing into the now-empty dockmaster's office. Papers and other debris floated about.

BULLS, HORNS, YOU KNOW THE DRILL

By the time the elevator doors parted, Scarlet was back to her seated position in the wheelchair.

As the elevator opened one level up and Scarlet rolled toward the Ops Center, Oracle reported, "The other boat is almost here. One hundred yards and closing. Two of the men have what appear to be boarding hooks at the ready. The storm has also intensified. I estimate we are an hour or two from its full force."

Scarlet rolled into her Secure Enclave, and as her little nook closed around her, she said, "Let's give them something to think about. Deploy the guns." She looked at another screen. "Nothing from the others? Emmett can't fly in this weather. Shit."

As loud clunks and whirs echoed from the fore and aft of the *Raven,* Oracle said, "Correct, we have received no transmissions from the others. I could attempt to directly control the drone myself. Guns deployed."

The screens surrounding Scarlet came to life, one with a split view of the gun camera from each of the two auto cannons.

The views tracked slowly back and forth until homing in on the approaching boat. Scarlet shook her head. "No, too risky. Let's solve our problems first, then deal with theirs." She reached for one of her keyboards and tapped a command. "Hey there, other boat. I'm on the boat you're heading toward. It's just me over here. I took out your pals—" a coughing sound came from the overhead speaker "—*We* took out your pals. They're tied up in a storeroom. By now you've noticed my two very shiny auto cannons. They're locked on to your craft and I'm guessing it would take ten seconds or less to shred your boat. Come to a stop and cut your engines, now."

On the display, the approaching boat was still approaching, now only eighty or so meters away, rising and falling on the swells kicked up by the storm as the wind raged against both vessels. It didn't seem to be any better at handling the storm than the *Raven*. Scarlet looked at the targeting displays. "I warned you. You can see the guns—do you think they're decorative?" she asked no one in particular. She pressed a control, and the bow-mounted auto cannon adjusted and opened fire tracking as both boats rose and fell.

The line of armor-piercing rounds stitched across the bow of the other boat, ripping holes in it. The fire continued past the boat, sending geysers of water ten feet into the air. The boat listed, and when its bow dipped, it went deeper into the water than before and didn't bounce back with as much buoyancy as before. She could see smoke coming from the ruined bow. Several pieces of metal and fiberglass fell into the water.

"They have cut their engines," Oracle reported, then added, "and they might be sinking."

Scarlet shrugged. "Mess with the bull, horns...you know the thing."

"I, in fact, do not. There are no livestock aboard the *Raven*. I cannot be certain about the other boat, however," the AI replied. Scarlet looked at the ceiling, but said nothing, choosing to detach from her technological cocoon and head for the bridge.

SIXTEEN

I'VE GOT THE POWER

When Jason looked through the doorway leading back into the main complex, he spotted Niles and Asako with their captor Phillipe Bouchard. A makeshift bandage around the small Asian woman's shoulder. He turned back to Sofia. "Found the reason for that gun shot earlier"

She leaned past Jason to get a look for herself and growled, "Why'd he shoot the professor?" She turned and looked at Jason. "I count six."

"See our gear?"

"Yup, on one of the small desks, next to what might be a hundred-plus-year-old bento box." She tapped her chin. "I bet that'd be worth a fortune."

Jason smiled. "Probably." He turned to the door. "So. Thoughts?"

Before the tall ex-marine could answer, the base shook, again.

Jason stepped away from the doorway. "That's like the fifth time or something. Something isn't right here." He looked back to the doorway and pointed. "I don't think there were cracks in this wall before."

Sofia knelt down and ran a finger along one of the cracks, at least a quarter-inch wide. She hummed to herself briefly. "You're right." The base shook again, and dust puffed out of the now-slightly-wider crack. "Definitely no bueno," she murmured.

Outside the security corridor, Bouchard, Niles, Asako, and the mercenaries were shouting at each other.

"Why would she know what's going on?" Niles growled, putting a protective arm in front of Asako as two of Bouchard's men aimed their rifles at her. He made sure to not bump her wounded shoulder.

"Because," Bouchard said, "she's the expert."

Asako tutted, "Expert? I am no such thing. I am a professor of East Asia studies. I stumbled onto this base while going over old World War Two documents released by the Japanese military. I know nothing of this place. No one does!" She shouted the last part.

"Unfortunate," the Frenchman replied, motioning for his men to lower their weapons. He turned to them. "Something is obviously happening that wasn't before. I suspect whatever it is, we won't like it." He motioned to himself, his men, and his prisoners to indicate the very royal *we*. "Let us work together to figure it out, oui?" When neither prisoner moved he added, "I trust I don't need to remind you of my seriousness?"

Niles and Asako traded looks before the large South African man nodded. "Very well, Mr. Bouchard. Why don't you fill us in on your group's doings since arriving here?" When the Frenchman looked like he was about to protest the implications, Niles continued, "It is reasonable to assume your men did something since the tremors began after you arrived." He pointed to the lights. "After the lights came on, specifically." His look said *challenge me on this*. Bouchard did not.

Bouchard motioned toward a door in the wall apart from everything else. No desks were near the door. It was in the same wall as the main entrance door. "The generator is through there. Let us take a look." He gestured for his remaining three men to surround Asako and Niles and then headed for the nondescript entrance. The petite academic was beginning to get pale.

The tunnel leading to the power plant of the ancient facility was not very long. Being set in the same wall as the entrance meant it was deeper under the hill they had built the base into and beneath. The sound of the over one-hundred-year-old generator was audible from outside the doorway. The faint smell of exhaust was also evident. Likely, whatever the base used to remove the generator's exhaust had become compromised in the intervening years. How the Japanese military kept the relatively small population of the island from spotting the exhaust or smelling it was beyond Niles, though certainly something he was curious about. It was likely one of many things he might not get an answer to.

The generator room was bigger than Niles expected. He and Asako both slowed as they entered in order to take in the space. Asako leaned against the rough hewn doorway. The ceiling was higher than any other in the base, including the sub bay, and what looked like small tunnels or vents had been drilled into the distant ceiling. Those tunnels must have led to small openings all over the hill, possibly the island. Wires ran to each opening. "They must have installed exhaust fans somewhere in each of the vents to help pull the exhaust out," Niles said to no one in particular as he stared up at the holes.

Bouchard looked at two of his men. "Go back into the main

section, and check on Bernard and the others in the barracks." He turned to Niles to ask, "You mentioned knowing what this base was for?"

ONE, TWO, PUNCH

The moment Bouchard and the rest of his men led Niles and Asako through the door to wherever the corridor beyond went, Jason and Sofia dashed to the desk where their weapons and equipment lay.

Jason looked at Sofia. "We need to secure the door to the barracks." The tall ex-marine withdrew a coil of what looked like rope. Jason smiled. "That'd do it." He turned and trotted back to the security corridor and the door to the barracks.

The coil was a special putty-like substance that Jason had created. Once pressed against the door and the frame and given a bit of current, like from sticking a nine-volt battery into it, it formed a powerful adhesive resin. Jason stood up and inspected his work, the nine-volt battery now essentially permanently attached to the door and door frame. "Okay, let's go get reacquainted with our French pal." Jason headed back into the main base complex.

Sofia and Jason were five feet from the door that led to the base's power plant when two men strode out, weapons held casually, aimed at the ground. Four pairs of eyes locked on to each other, and for a second no one moved until a blur that very much looked like a brown-skinned ex-marine tackled one of the stunned mercenaries. Jason and the still-standing mercenary watched Sofia, then looked at each other for another second before either could muster themselves to motion. The mercenary was slightly faster, lunging at Jason and closing the distance before Jason could do anything but raise his arms in the air protectively, assuming the man was about to punch him in the face. In fact, the mercenary was more interested in tackling Jason and forcing him to the ground, which he did.

Jason let out a loud oof as he hit the stone floor. Remembering the moves Sofia drilled into him daily when back at the Expedition, Inc., office, he forced a knee up between him and the other man, while also doing his best to cover the man's mouth in case he shouted for help. The other man landed several blows to Jason's midsection before Jason could find the right leverage to kick the man off of him. He rolled and got to his feet a split second after the merc. Not wasting a moment, he let fly a kick to the other man's groin that doubled his opponent over. "Not fair," the man groaned as tears ran down his cheeks. Jason leaned in to land a right cross, knocking the mercenary out.

From a few feet away, Sofia released the man she had in a triangle choke with her legs. His limp form rolled to the side, away from her. "Nicely done." She nodded approvingly. Jason bowed. She pointed to the doorway. "Let's go get our nerds."

* * *

"They were working on biological weapons," Asako said through gritted teeth before Niles had a chance. She was sweating.

Bouchard's eyebrows shot up. "Do tell." He looked around. "Is this place dangerous?"

Niles took over. "So far the danger has only come from you and your men." He growled. When his captor just stared at him blankly, he added. "We do not know. But from what Asako read in the journals she found on the sub, it has likely long since gone inert."

The Frenchman inhaled slowly. "I see. That is most certainly unexpected."

Asako nodded. "Understatement of the century, Mr. Bouchard." Another tremor rumbled through the base. "But that seems the least of our worries."

Niles had moved to inspect something and turned to the others. "Look here." Bouchard, Asako, and the lone mercenary came over. "Does this look like a timer to anyone else?" The device he was pointing at was rusty and covered in nearly an inch of dust. Wires ran out both sides, one side leading to the electrical panel on the generator. The bundle of wires coming from the other side of the device ran into a small conduit that likely led back into the base proper, somewhere. Niles hummed as he knelt to further inspect the device, blowing on it to clear the dust. "The engineering of this base is amazing," he said out loud but to himself. Asako rolled her eyes at her friend's use of his favorite adjective. It felt good to, for a second, forget about her gunshot wound. Niles brushed at the front of the device, exposing a grimy glass cover. Dials with digits on them were slowly spinning. Counting down.

WELL, THIS WENT SOUTH FAST

"Hello, Frenchie," Jason said as he entered the power plant, pistol held in front of him, aimed at Bouchard. Sofia entered and hurried to remove Bouchard's and his mercenary's weapons. "You two okay?" Jason asked, making eye contact with Asako and Niles. His South African friend nodded vigorously. Asako nodded once, slowly. Sofia moved quickly to the small woman's side to inspect the wound.

Niles showed the timing device. "Jason, we have a problem." As if to emphasize the point, another tremor rumbled through the base, this one causing everyone in the room to glance around as dust and several baseball-sized rocks fell from the ceiling. Niles pointed to the dusty timing device.

From the radio on Bouchard's belt, a voice said, "Boss, they flood the sub bay!"

Everyone turned to look first at the radio, then its owner. Jason motioned for the Frenchman to answer. Bouchard raised the radio, "What do you mean? Everyone report in."

"This is Chin. I went to check that office with the tunnel and water is rushing up out of the opening."

244

"Merde," Bouchard hissed, then looked at Jason, one eyebrow raised.

Jason ignored the Frenchman and looked at Niles, who pointed to the device next to him, the spinning dials still counting down. "I believe that restoring power restored power to whatever this primitive timer is. Some type of self-destruct is my guess, based on the evidence." The heavyset man raised his hands in an *all of this* gesture.

Jason rubbed his face with his free hand. "Can you stop it?"

"Boss?" the radio in Bouchard's hand said. The Frenchman again raised an eyebrow as he stared at Jason.

"Tell your men to meet you in the science lab," Jason said, then waved his pistol in a go-ahead motion.

"Meet me in the science labs," Bouchard said into the radio, then added quickly, "Code seven." Jason lunged and snatched the radio from the man's hands. The Frenchman was grinning.

Sofia groaned as the radio in Jason's hand erupted with mercenaries checking in, several announcing that they had been trapped in the barracks.

Before anyone else could comment, a loud crack came from somewhere inside the base, the sound echoing around the rock facility. Jason strode toward Niles, pushing him out of the way. He quickly took aim and shot the timing device twice, utterly destroying it. Sparks, springs, and pieces of dials with numbers painted on them flew in all directions. A piece of plastic with 4 printed on it landed on his shoe. He turned to the others and shrugged. "Can't hurt?" He motioned Bouchard and his man. "Let's go. I think escaping might not be a bad idea right now. We can regroup topside and see what's going on, make contact with the Raven, maybe the authorities." He glared at Bouchard. The Frenchman shrugged.

Outside the entrance to the power generation room, the

mercenaries not locked in rooms had gathered and were looking around more than a little worried. Water was gurgling out of the office bloc now, rushing toward the opposite wall from the entrance to the power generation room. The floor of the base exhibited a tilt it didn't have when they entered, several hours ago.

Sofia emerged from the tunnel, rifle up and ready. Every mercenary in the room spun almost simultaneously, their own weapons snapping up to take aim. Before she could say anything, Bouchard emerged with Jason standing right behind him, Jason's pistol pointed as his temple. Sofia grinned. "Drop 'em."

Jason wiggled his pistol. "You heard her, gentlemen. Drop your weapons." He pushed the pistol against Bouchard's head. "Now."

The mercenaries did as instructed, glaring at Jason and the others. Before anyone could say anything, another tremor rumbled through the base. This one lasted longer than the ones previous.

"That didn't sound or feel good," Jason said, glancing at Niles.

The heavyset South African half shrugged, one arm holding up Asako. "Perhaps the destruction of the timer did not stop whatever process it was managing. Or perhaps the self-destruct process has already progressed beyond a point at which it can stop." He glanced around and then pointed. The far side of the base was filling with water. A loud crack echoed through the space as the floor dropped several inches. The pre-fab walls of the office bloc collapsed, and water surged up through a much larger hole than had originally been the tunnel to the sub bay.

"Holy hell! This is going south fast!" Jason yelled over the sound of the water rushing into the space. The wall that separated the main complex from the security corridor collapsed next. Loud bangs came from the door that led to the barracks. He and Sofia glanced at each other. "Uh, a few of your men are trapped in there," Jason said, pointing to the sealed door.

STORM'S A COMIN'

THE STORM HAD FINALLY FULLY ARRIVED IN THE MASSET Inlet. The *Raven* was being tossed all over the place. It was all Scarlet could do to keep the boat slowly moving in the shore's direction, the shore that Jason and the others had headed for hours ago. It was slow going, but she was at least putting some distance between the *Raven* and the other boat.

"Scarlet, based on data from the Canadian weather service, this storm is approximately ten miles wide," Oracle reported from the ceiling.

"Shit, big one," the hacker said as she worked several keyboards at once. Thankfully, she had slaved all the *Raven*'s controls to her workstation, ensuring she didn't have to venture to the bridge, which was likely being lashed with rain and had next to no visibility. She glanced at her watch. "Should be sunrise soon. That'll help." She looked at another display showing a map with the storm on it. "I think."

The *Raven* groaned as she rose and fell over swells. Down in the storage closet, the captured mercenaries were doing their best to keep their stomachs under control. Their leader, Lanh, was banging on the door and shouting to be released. Without warning, the door opened in, sending Lanh sprawling to the floor with his men. Rufus was standing in the doorway, stunner raised. From a speaker somewhere in his fake flesh and mechanical body, Oracle said, "Please refrain from making so much noise."

"Release us!" Lanh shouted.

"I am afraid that is not an option at the moment. A severe storm has arrived, and the inlet is tremendously choppy," Oracle replied through Rufus. The *Raven* plunged, causing the stomachs of everyone in the room to lurch. Rufus didn't budge. "For your own safety, please remain calm." Rufus reached for the door as the *Raven* lurched again, first up then suddenly down. The mechanical construct lost its footing, stumbling into the room a step. It was all Lanh needed. He rushed the mechanical construct with enough force to further destabilize the automaton. The other mercenaries made their move, following their leader. They rushed past Rufus, pushing him into the room. "Stop, please stop right there," Oracle urged from the speaker inside Rufus.

"Scarlet, we have a situation," Oracle said from the speaker in the Ops Center.

"Oh, goody." She glanced at the bank of monitors around her, spotting the now-freed mercenaries rushing through the corridor the deck above. "What the hell? How'd you let them out?"

"They were making a tremendous amount of noise. I was concerned."

"Concerned about the bad guys?" Scarlet ran her hands through her hair, then tightened her ponytail. "They're the bad guys. We don't waste cycles concerned about the bad guys." She looked up at the speaker. "Make a reminder: when we get home, we need to go over some basic ground rules."

"Okay, done. I am sorry, Scarlet."

"Let's just keep 'em from taking over the boat," Scarlet replied, watching the men take the stairs to the main deck.

"I have secured the bridge and disconnected the control interfaces up there, just in case," Oracle said.

Scarlet nodded. "Good call."

"I have also been able to get Rufus back up and running," the IA replied hopefully.

SEVENTEEN

THAT'S A LOT OF WATER

WATER BUBBLED OUT FROM UNDER THE SEALED DOOR leading to the barracks. "That's probably not good," Jason said, standing behind several mercenaries as they tried to force the door. Their comrades on the other side were still banging loudly on it.

Bouchard looked from Jason to Sofia. "How do we open it?" He was careful to not move too quickly as Sofia still had her rifle trained on him.

Jason looked at Niles and shrugged. He turned to the men working on the door. "Out of the way." They turned and looked at Bouchard, who also shrugged but nodded for them to let Jason pass. Jason withdrew a small cylinder from his satchel and sprayed the long bead of adhesive resin he'd applied earlier. The mercenaries stared intently, and at first, nothing happened. Then, without warning, the line of putty he'd applied to seal the door hissed and spit, bubbles forming on its previously hard glossy surface. One of the mercs turned to Jason only to be met with a smile and a shrug. Jason pointed to the door. It took about forty-five seconds for the chemical he'd applied to do its job.

The now malleable resin ran to the floor in sticky globs. With a wet squishing sound, the door opened, goop stretching between frame and door. Jason grabbed the nine-volt battery off the ground. "I don't like to waste," he said, pocketing the battery. Bouchard looked at him but said nothing, eyebrow arched.

The first through the door was the large African mercenary that Jason and Sofia had met earlier. He saw Jason and immediately charged him, wrapping his enormous hands around Jason's neck. Jason slammed his palms on the much larger man's much larger biceps to no avail. The other mercenaries had all turned to watch the spectacle. Bouchard stood and smiled, saying nothing.

Sofia watched, smiling to herself, until Jason's eyes locked on to hers. "Fine," she sighed and raised her rifle, firing a single round into the ceiling. A tremor rumbled through the base. Something in one of the other rooms gave a loud boom. Everyone spun to look at Sofia, including the mercenary choking Jason, who let her boss go. "What? I didn't do that!" She waved to encompass the recently shaken base. She motioned with her rifle at the large, angry mercenary that had recently been throttling Jason. "Step back."

Bouchard coughed. "Perhaps we leave this rather wet party, oui?"

Niles looked down at Asako still limply leaning on him, mostly supported by his arm now. "Yes, let's. She doesn't look good." He glared at Bouchard.

Another loud snap echoed through the base, as an actual crack shot through the floor from the direction of the barracks and science labs to the entrance. The entire room shook, and the door to the barracks collapsed as a large stone beam fell across it.

Asako looked around. "This place is falling apart!" Her pale face betrayed her dismay. Before anyone could reply, she darted toward the ruined security corridor and the door to the science labs with strength that a minute ago she didn't appear to have.

"The fuck?!" Jason hissed. He looked at Niles, then Sofia, then to Bouchard. He pointed at Sofia, then the Frenchman. "Watch him." He motioned to the gathered mercenaries standing around. "Them."

Sofia nodded. She reached into her belt and withdrew a pistol, handing it to Niles. "Hurry," she said, gesturing with her head toward the doorway and rising water near it. Another tremor shook the ground, followed by more loud cracks. Several mercenaries shouted. Jason ran for the door Asako had vanished through.

Asako emerged into the science labs and looked around, her eyes blinking rapidly as she scanned the room. Her damaged shoulder bleeding anew. The repeated tremors had overturned several of the stainless-steel tables; others had slid around the room. She moved from table to table, lifting papers, shuffling items around with her good hand.

"Asako, this is dangerous," Jason said from the doorway. "This place is collapsing and, well, so are you."

"We have to preserve what we can!" She stumbled from one table to another as if looking for something. She looked at the table's contents as she leaned heavily on it.

"What are you looking for?" Jason asked, trotting over to her as another tremor shook the base.

"Anything!" she shouted as she grabbed a folder and shoved it into her backpack. Jason moved to join her, but she lurched toward another workstation.

A crack shot through the wall. Water ran out, first a trickle, but it was increasing in flow rapidly. Asako looked at the crack and ran to a workstation near it as water splashed onto the top, drenching papers. "No!" she hissed, wincing.

Jason watched, then shrugged and moved to one of the far workstations. "Two minutes!" he shouted over the sound of water flowing freely into the room.

DO ISLANDS SINK?

THE STANDOFF IN THE MAIN COMPLEX WAS GETTING TENSE, Sofia and Niles versus Bouchard and a dozen mercenaries. Niles was sweeping the room with his pistol. "Where are they?" He was pretty proud that his hand wasn't shaking very much.

The Hispanic woman shrugged. "Same place they were—" She didn't finish because a fracture shot through the floor and immediately widened, going from nothing to a chasm of over five feet in under a minute. The light strands along the ceiling snapped as the room stretched beyond their length. "Mierda!" Sofia shouted as two of the mercenaries fell into the gap, their screams dying out with *thuds* as they hit the bottom.

"Merde!" Bouchard shouted, stepping back, grabbing the collar of one of his men as he teetered on the ledge. The base trembled, but unlike before, the shaking didn't stop. The base was coming apart.

"ASAKO, WE HAVE TO GO!" JASON SHOUTED AS THE ROOM shook. This time the shaking did not stop. One of the light fixtures fell from the ceiling, nearly striking Asako, who staggered clear, barely. The crack in the wall turned into a geyser as it widened and stretched to the floor, splitting it. Jason sprinted toward Asako and jumped over the crack that was widening by the minute. "Now!" he shouted when he landed. The petite Asian professor was still frantically grabbing papers and other bits and pieces from workstations, seeming to ignore Jason. He grabbed her shoulder and spun her to face him. "Now! This place is collapsing! We have to go, or we'll be trapped!" Her scream of pain reminded him that he had grabbed her injured shoulder. The rumble of rock scraping on rock was growing louder and louder.

Whatever trance had taken over her broke, and Asako blinked rapidly as she looked up at and sagged against Jason. "Okay, yes. Let's go," she rasped, grabbing a stack of papers from the desk nearest her and shoving them into her backpack.

Jason turned back to the way they'd come in. The doorway was still intact, but the tunnel looked collapsed, at least partially. "Shit!" Jason hissed. He turned to Asako. "Come on!" Holding her hand, he ran toward the fissure in the middle of the room. He could have cleared the opening without a running start but wasn't sure about his much shorter companion. He toggled his short-range radio. "Anyone hear me? The tunnel looks to have collapsed."

"—son? The tunnel? — 're okay?" It sounded like Niles.

"Niles, yeah we're fine, but the labs are coming apart! There's a split in the floor and water is rushing in from somewhere."

"Okay, we— ing. Hold ti—" came the garbled reply.

Jason looked at Asako. "Let's see what we can move on this side." She nodded.

From the short range comm in Niles' ear came, "Anyone — me? — tunnel looks — collapsed." He pressed his palm over his ear to try to hear better. "Jason? The tunnel? You're okay?"

The low power comms they used to avoid being picked up by nearby sources didn't do well with stuff in the way. Collapsing rocks and water both held places very high on the list of things that interfered with the comms. Jason replied, "Niles, — fine, but — are coming apart! — a split in the floor and — rushing in from some—."

Niles looked at Sofia, whom he knew was listening. "Okay, we're coming. Hold tight!" He turned to Bouchard. "Have your men help us."

The Frenchman spread his arms, palms up. "And why would I do that, mon bon professeur?"

Sofia moved closer, raising her rifle, the look on her face was explanation enough. Bouchard shrugged and motioned to the remains of the security corridor. "You heard the professor. Let's go see if we can't save Mr. Kincaid and Ms. ...?" He looked at Niles, who said, "Yamamoto." She nodded, "Ms. Yamamoto." The mercenaries glared at Sofia and Niles but headed in the indicated direction. Sofia motioned for Bouchard to follow as she and Niles fell in behind him.

The slight tilt of the floor nearest the door to the sub bay had grown extremely pronounced. Water had filled half the room, and the door to the sub bay couldn't be seen.

As the mercenaries got to work in the short tunnel that led to the science labs, forming a fire brigade line to remove the stone, a large bang echoed. Sofia and Bouchard looked up as the ceiling over the large fissure gave way, splitting wide open to reveal a ten-meter rock canyon and what must have been the sky above. It was hard to tell, since the sky above was pitch black, broken only occasionally by bright lightning bolts.

ONE SHOT

"Scarlet, the other boat is definitely sinking," Oracle said as Scarlet watched the now-freed mercenaries ransack the main lounge. Two of them, Lanh included, had attempted to take control of the bridge but found it useless. The few consoles they could figure out how to access showed network and control interface errors. Most of the panels refused to power up at all.

In the corner of the room was a pile of sub-machine guns and pistols. "Glad we brought their guns in here," Scarlet said as she turned her attention to another monitor. On it, the other boat was rising and falling, much like the *Raven* was in the storm swells. Unlike the *Raven*, the other vessel seemed to be listing to starboard by at least ten, maybe fifteen degrees and wasn't bouncing nearly as much as the *Raven*. Scarlet rubbed her chin. "Are they in danger of sinking?"

"It is impossible to be certain with the limited data at hand, but I assume that no, they are not in immediate danger." Before Scarlet could comment, Oracle continued, "However, that could change quickly depending on how long this storm lasts or how severe the internal damage might be. Or how skilled the pilot is."

Scarlet said nothing for a few seconds, thinking, then looked between the monitor showing the other boat and the view of the mercenaries in the lounge. "Okay, we gotta get these buttheads off the *Raven* and, if possible, maybe save the other boat. Thoughts?"

Oracle took long enough to reply that Scarlet opened her mouth to make sure the AI was working on the problem. Before the young hacker could say a word, Oracle finally said, "Using Rufus we could guide the mercenaries to the boat launch. I can inflate the emergency tender and they can take it over to their boat."

Scarlet nodded slowly. "How does that help keep their boat from sinking?"

"We can provide an inflatable bladder. They can place it in the forward section where the hull damage is most significant."

Scarlet snapped her fingers. "That's a great idea! I forgot we had one of those on board!" She looked down at her lap. "How do we get it to the tender?"

"Rufus."

The *Raven* rocked violently, causing Scarlet's stomach to feel like she'd left it ten feet above her head. "I think this storm will get a bit worse before it gets better." She glanced at the screen showing the lounge. "Here's the plan: get Rufus moving. It's going to take him a bit to get the bladder. He's not the nimblest of guys. I'll go lead our friends to the tender." She looked at the ceiling. "Get it inflated and ready to launch."

"Are you sure that is a good idea, Scarlet? Those men are likely quite dangerous, even unarmed." Oracle sounded worried.

"Not in the least, but I don't know if the other boat has time for Rufus' slow ass to meander up and down the boat trying to do it all." She pressed the button to release her from her workstation, panels folding out of the way as her chair was freed. "Make it so."

"Acknowledged."

One deck above the Ops Center, Rufus came to life, leaving the storage closet he was standing in, the one that previously held the mercenaries. He marched into the waiting elevator and went down one level. The doors opened to a waiting Scarlet, who rolled to the side to allow the lumbering mechanism to pass as she entered the lift. Rufus marched toward the bow of the ship and a large cargo hold.

The elevator made a ding sound, causing all four mercenaries to spin. One had a rolling pin stolen from the kitchenette in his hand. The doors parted to reveal Scarlet. "Come with me if you want to live," she said. The mercenaries stared at her, slack jawed. She motioned into the small elevator car. "Well? Come on!" The *Raven* lurched sideways, sending two of the mercenaries sprawling to the deck. Scarlet sighed. "Come on!"

Below decks, Rufus was in the cargo hold attempting to grasp a three-foot-wide plastic storage crate, while not losing his balance. It was taking a significant amount of processing power for Oracle to guide the ungainly monster as the *Raven* lurched all over the place.

"Why should we trust you?" Lanh asked, eyeing her suspiciously. His hands flexed into fists.

"Because your boat is sinking. Or at least damaged and taking on water. I don't want you here on the *Raven*, so I'm sending you home in our emergency tender. Along with an inflatable bladder that should at least keep your boat from taking on more water." The *Raven* rose several feet into the air before slamming back down the backside of the swell. Scarlet made a face, "Time ain't on your side, man, come on!" Lanh thought for a moment, then motioned for his men to join him in the elevator.

PART 5

EIGHTEEN

COLLAPSE

"I SEE THEM!" ONE OF THE MERCENARIES SHOUTED, turning to look at Bouchard and Sofia.

The base had continued to fill with water. For the moment, the massive fissure that had opened in the floor was keeping the water from reaching the two teams of people. Where that water was going no one seemed to want to know. That couldn't last forever, though, Sofia assumed as she watched several square feet of wall and ceiling fall into the water. While Bouchard's men had been removing rubble, she'd ventured over to the fissure. Most of the lights had gone out and even though her night vision goggles were amazing, she couldn't make heads or tails of what she was seeing below the floor of the base.

"I believe this base is, in fact, built into a natural cave," Niles said, joining her. The base shook, more violently than it had before. The wall with the entrance to the sub bay fell away completely. Where the wall and much of the floor had been not that long ago was a gaping chasm with what looked like three-foot-thick pillars, or what remained of them, spaced every ten or so feet. Niles pointed. "Some type of stonework suspension system, also likely part of the self-destruct system our French friend inadvertently re-activated." He could see stone pins in several of the more intact pillars. Each had some sort of explosive device attached to it. The not-intact pillars all seemed to have split where the pin would have been, then spiraled apart along a pre-cut channel. "Ingenious," he muttered.

From the direction of the science labs, Jason shouted, "Okay, time to go, everyone!" He and Asako were soaking wet and covered in dust turned to mud.

Sofia turned and saw her friend and employer dirt and grime covered as he was trotting toward the entrance, their client Asako Yamamoto's hand in his. The small Asian woman was as much being dragged as she was keeping up. Her injured shoulder was a mix of blood and dirt.

When they came to a stop, the small Asian woman withdrew her hand. "I know how to walk without help," she snapped then wavered. Niles moved in to support is his old colleague. Jason looked at her, then focused on the rest of the group.

Bouchard was hot on their heels, his men behind him. Niles and Sofia exchanged a look and moved to follow. As Jason reached the entrance, a loud crack boomed, and the remaining base complex shook. The floor tilted, and the entrance collapsed, then shifted away from the tunnel it was connected to. Shouts and screams filled the rapidly shifting space. Sofia glanced to her right and spied the entrance to the power generation room. Without a word, she shoved Niles toward the for-the-moment intact doorway. "Jason!" she screamed as the floor tilted more. Jason spun on his heels and flung Asako over his shoulder. Bouchard saw what was happening and turned. Jason, Asako over his shoulder, cleared the threshold just as the floor separated from the doorway. The remains of the office section of the centuries-old base tilted away as stone pillars gave way beneath. Bouchard's men were scattered. Some had jumped for the ruined entrance only to slide screaming down the rocky face of the natural cave the base had been fit inside of. The Frenchman jumped as the base continued to slide away from the door. If Jason hadn't moved, the foreign privateer would have slammed into a wall of people and joined his men fifty feet below in the water, rocks falling down on them.

The five people in the tunnel leading to the power generation room watched as the last of the pillars finally gave way, allowing the entire Japanese base to fall to the cave floor below, water churning angrily as tons of rock and office furniture fell into it. The far side of the cave showed the remains of the tunnel to the sub bay, water flowing out of it in a waterfall. The science labs and barracks, built partially into the cave wall, were the last to collapse and fall, portions of each remaining in the cavern's wall.

As things quieted, another loud rumble began. "What now?" Jason wondered aloud, looking around. The ceiling, compromised as it was and with rain pouring through the large wound it had suffered, sloughed away. Top soil, trees, and massive boulders tumbled into the void. Jason spun and pushed everyone deeper inside the power plant room. The ancient generator was still somehow running. The exhaust tunnels having collapsed, the room was filling with noxious fumes.

"Shut it off!" screamed Sofia.

"Where's the kill switch?" Jason shouted, his eyes clamped shut, hands outstretched, feeling his way along the wall.

Someone said something in French. The loud chugging of the generator stopped.

BUH BYE

Lanh and the mercenaries required no further convincing once they arrived in the launch bay in the aft section of the *Raven*. The emergency tender was nearly inflated when they arrived. "Once that's inflated and Rufus brings the bladder, you can go," Scarlet said from the corner of the room. The mercenaries were already piling into the tender, waiting for it to finish.

Lanh turned to the wheelchair-bound young woman. "Why are you doing this?"

"Because I'm the one that shot up your boat, so this is partly my fault." She held up a hand when he opened his mouth to respond. "Also, we don't take prisoners. I didn't want you on the *Raven*. We're also not cruel." Her face made it clear she didn't need or want him to reply. The man just nodded and turned to his men.

The hatch opened and a large ruggedized storage case pushed its way into the launch bay on two monstrous mechanical and flesh legs. Two of the mercenaries released very un-mercenary sounding shrieks before realizing it was the robot they'd encountered before. Scarlet stifled a chuckle, knowing it wouldn't help the tense situation. Rufus trundled over and not at all gracefully deposited the storage case in the tender. Scarlet rolled closer to the edge of the loading area. "When you get to your ship, take the bladder out of the case, put it as far forward as possible with the control unit as far from the damage as possible, then press the big green button."

"What will happen then?" Lanh asked as he motioned one of his men to sit near the engine.

"The bladder is super malleable and will inflate rapidly to fill the space. It'll push into every hole in the hull. It won't stop inflating until it reaches a certain amount of resistance." She snapped her fingers. "Oh yeah, close the door and secure it behind you when it deploys; otherwise, it'll try to fill the corridor. It'll fill aggressively and go where there is the least resistance," she added. Without waiting for the man to acknowledge, she looked at the control panel on the wall. "Ready? Opening bay." She pressed a button and the back of the room split, then slowly tilted up as it split open. The floor lowered slightly as the space around the tender filled with water.

As the emergency tender pushed back out of the *Raven*, Lanh looked over to Scarlet and nodded. She returned the gesture and waited until the small craft cleared the lip of the bay before pressing the button to close up the aft section of the *Raven*. She looked at Rufus, then the ceiling. "Go ahead and put Rufus away. I don't think we'll need him anymore."

The automaton turned and made its way out of the launch bay. From the ceiling, Oracle replied, "Acknowledged."

As the launch bay doors closed and the automatic pump cleared the water out of the lower area, Scarlet took a deep breath and blew it out loudly. She turned and headed for the hatch that Rufus had just taken. The *Raven* lurched and tilted, making sure that Scarlet knew that the storm was still raging.

THE FIRST STEP IS A DOOZY

THE STORM THAT HAD UNTIL RECENTLY BEEN RAGING impotently outside the Japanese base was now raging fully inside the ruins of the base. From the doorway of the power plant was an almost unobstructed view of the island to the inlet.

"We have to get out of here!" Jason shouted over the wind.

Sofia, who'd taken to guarding Phillipe Bouchard, nodded. "Sí!" She looked past Jason to the drop behind him. "Ideas?"

Before Jason could answer, Asako did. "What if we climb down?" She was so quiet and weak she had to repeat herself. She pointed past Jason to the chasm that had previously held the Japanese base but now was a mess of smashed concrete blocks and pillars. Several pillars somehow were still standing, rising several dozen feet out of the churning water below.

Jason rubbed his chin, peering over the edge. "Fifty-foot drop. I can't imagine that water is over ten feet deep. Lotta rubble, too." He looked at the others. "I don't think jumping is a good idea."

Bouchard coughed, and when all eyes turned to him, he pointed to a pile of wires. Wires that previously fed the light strands and power trunks running to the rest of the base but had snapped as the base collapsed.

Jason looked at Sofia, who shrugged and said, "As good an idea as any." She looked over to Bouchard, who grinned and rocked on his heels. Sofia scowled.

Lightning cracked overhead, and off to the side, a piece of the base that had been teetering finally gave up and fell, tumbling into the water and rubble below, throwing geysers of water into the air.

"Yeah, okay," Jason said, heading for the pile of wires. "Let's do this."

Niles bent down to help Jason with the wires and mumbled, "Such a horrible waste."

Jason glanced at his friend. "The base or those mercs?"

Niles scoffed, "The base, though it's a shame so many men had to die." The heavyset man looked over his shoulder at their French guest. "Though they made their choices."

Jason hefted a bundle of wire. "Indeed." He stood and walked to the edge of the doorway that used to lead into the Japanese base and tossed it over. The heavy-duty wire cascaded down the side of the cavern—or more accurately now, the valley—that used to house the Japanese base.

The wire made it almost to the water. Jason looked down, barely able to see the cable in the false light of his night vision goggles. The storm overhead was lessening, but the wind and rain were still battering them. He turned to the group. "Okay, Sofia goes, then Niles, Frenchie, and I'll bring up the rear with Asako."

"I have a name," Bouchard replied, but Jason held a hand up to silence the Frenchman.

Jason withdrew his pistol as Sofia slung her rifle over her shoulder and leaned out over the edge. "Fun," she said, barely loud enough to be heard. She reached down, grabbed the hefty cable, and began her descent.

As Sofia began her descent, Jason's comm crackled, "—one there? Jas— fia? Niles?" He placed a hand to his ear. "Scarlet? Is that you? Signal is very weak."

"—son! Thank God. I was wor— creepy French— you," Scarlet's static-filled reply came back.

Jason glanced at Bouchard. "Well, we did meet a Frenchman. Long story. Are you okay? Is the Raven okay?"

"— okay, some clean— ed but otherwise ship— The other boat — might — tow," Scarlet replied. Jason leaned over the edge to see that Sofia had dropped that last few feet into the water. The Ex-Marine had found a handhold in the remains of one of the pillars. He looked over to Niles. "Your turn."

The big South African academic trotted to the edge, looked over, then turned to Jason. "I could wait here."

Jason smiled and pointed to the cable that vanished over the edge. "Sooner you start climbing, sooner it's over."

The big man scowled but dropped to the ground and shimmied his way over the edge, a death grip on the cable. The generator made a slight groan in protest at supporting the weight of the heavyset archeologist. Jason looked at the machine and the cable before glancing at Bouchard. The Frenchman shrugged, then said, "Perhaps he should have gone last?" Jason extended the middle finger of his right hand, then motioned with his left hand, the hand holding the pistol, for Bouchard to head to the edge.

Once Niles dropped to the water and Bouchard had begun his climb, Jason looked at Asako, "This isn't going to be fun, for either of us." She had slumped down along the wall. She nodded and tried to stand. He helped her up, then slung her over his shoulder. "Hold on as tight as you can." He leaned over the edge and began his descent.

NINETEEN

HIGHER GROUND

"Now what?" Niles asked as the group bobbed in the water that had filled the natural cavern where the Japanese had built their base inside. He was doing his best to not only keep himself afloat, but to keep Asako above water as well.

Jason motioned toward the far side of the cavern. "I think we might be able to climb up over there." He looked over to Sofia. "You hear Scarlet? Sounds like she's okay."

Sofia started swimming in the specified direction. "That's good," she shouted over her shoulder. The others followed suit.

Jason looked at Bouchard. "Feel free to drown or get lost whenever it's convenient for you." He didn't wait for an answer as he increased his stroke to pull ahead.

The chasm that the Japanese had suspended the base over wasn't much larger than the base, so the swim to the opposite side didn't take long, even for someone like Niles, who wasn't very used to physical activity. As the group left the water, the rain let up. Asako looked up. "That's good. Looks like maybe the storm is breaking or at least passing." She looked east. "Sunrise."

Everyone turned. The sky that had until recently been an angry purple and filled with furious storm clouds had brightened. As the group trudged up the slope out of the ruins of the base, they could hear the faint but familiar sound of small propellers.

"Is that?" Niles asked.

"Emmett or whatever Scarlet calls it? Yes," Jason said, beaming.

"You guys read me?" Scarlet asked over comms. There was no static this time.

"Mi compañera, it's good to hear your voice," Sofia said, smiling for the first time in a day or two.

"Back atcha, Chica. It's great to hear your voice. Everyone is okay, right?" Scarlet asked.

"We're fine, dear," Niles answered. He looked at Asako. "All of us." The Asian woman smiled weakly. He added, "But prep the medbay, please. Asako has been shot." He turned and glared at Bouchard.

There was silence for a handful of heartbeats, "Copy that. And that creepy French butthead?" the hacker asked.

Jason turned to look at Bouchard. "He's here with us. His men—" Jason looked over his shoulder at the ruins of the base— "not so much."

"If they were anything like the ones he left aboard the Raven, the world is better off, I'm sure."

Jason's eyes narrowed as he turned back to Bouchard. "He left men on the Raven? How many? What happened?" The Frenchman shrugged and smiled, then picked up his pace to put some distance between himself and Jason. He groaned slightly when he realized he was now within striking distance of Sofia, who was on the same comm channel. She turned and growled.

"Long story, but the Raven is fine, I'm fine, everything is fine." She paused as if waiting for someone to acknowledge something, then continued, "Anyway, his men are back aboard their boat and it's stopped sinking, as far as Oracle can tell.

We've already put out a call to the Canadian authorities. They're pretty backed up, what with those two storms, but will get a cutter out here as soon as they can."

Jason nodded. "That's good to hear. I'm sure he'll be thrilled."

Overhead, the drone named Emmett came into view, its red and green lights blinking.

Niles looked at the others, then the drone. "I have never been happier to see one of Scarlet's toys in my life." Jason nodded and waved to the device.

"Lanh? Do you copy?" Bouchard said. Everyone spun to look at the man. He had a small radio in his hand.

Jason looked at Sofia and gestured to the Frenchman. "I thought you searched him?"

"Why would I have done that?" the tall Hispanic woman asked.

Jason's mouth hung open. "He could have a gun in one of those pockets!" He waved his hand toward Bouchard's cargo pants.

Bouchard put the radio down and reached into a thigh pocket. "I did." He withdrew a compact pistol. Jason snatched it out of his hands. "I did not feel the need to use it. I didn't think you posed a threat to my well-being." He smiled, then lifted the small radio. "Lanh, come in."

Jason looked at Sofia. "I'm so disappointed in you." She replied with a rude gesture.

BREAKFAST ALWAYS MAKES THINGS BETTER

The march back to the beach was uneventful, Jason ended up carrying Asako most of the way, her adrenaline finally giving way. Bouchard got in touch with his people, and when they arrived at the beach, he boarded the tender he and his men brought to shore. Once the small boat was underway, the Frenchman turned and waved, grinning as if he was leaving a group of friends after a day at the beach.

"I don't like that guy," Jason said as the team watched the tender motor away from shore toward a distinctly damaged boat a few hundred yards offshore. The *Raven* was sitting a hundred yards to port of the damaged boat, rocking gently in the post-storm swells slightly closer to shore.

Niles pointed up the beach a way. "Thankfully, our own ride is still where we left it." Sofia nodded. "I was a little worried it might have washed away in the storm."

"Fortune smiles on us," Asako mumbled, the tension of the previous days washing away from her. Niles rested a hand on her uninjured shoulder. They headed for the *Raven's* tender.

* * *

"Am I glad to see you guys!" Scarlet said from the railing of the *Raven's* launch bay. When she spotted Asako leaning against Nile, pale as a sheet, she gasped. The U-shaped raised deck wrapped around the tender. The outer doors were closing as the water drained from under the smaller craft. Jason climbed out, then awkwardly accepted Asako from Sofia. As soon as he had the small woman in his arms he headed for the exit. Sofia hopped out and helped Niles out of the small craft.

"I am glad to see you all alive and well, also," Oracle said from a speaker in the ceiling. "Scarlet and I had quite the adventure in your absence."

Niles smiled. "Yes, I'm sure you did." He looked at Scarlet, "Medbay is ready?"

Scarlet backed up to let everyone climb up and out of the shallow well the tender rested in. "Yeah, what happened? Who shot her?"

"That French prick," Sofia offered as she locked down the controls for the bay doors before exiting the room.

Niles patted Scarlet's shoulder. "Any word on the Canadian authorities?"

Scarlet shook her head. "Nope, they just said they'd get a cutter out ASAP. Eh." She smiled. "Oh, come on, that was funny!" She affected a face. "Eh."

They exited the elevator and started toward the medbay hatch. Niles looked at the mess Bouchard's men had made and groaned. The Medbay and Ops Center were on the same deck.

As they neared medbay Sofia said, "Well, from what I could see as we approached, Bouchard's boat isn't going anywhere, anytime soon."

As they reached the hatch Jason poked his head out, "Was that our emergency repair bladder I saw poking out of their bow? Our patent-still-pending emergency repair bladder?"

Sofia and Niles pushed passed him into the small medical center. He moved to stand in the corridor with Scarlet.

Scarlet blushed. "Yeah, I didn't know what else to do. I mean, they were probably going to founder, and you know, that's a lot of dead dudes on my conscience." She shuddered, "I'm not ready for that."

"Wuss," Sofia said from inside the medbay. Jason smiled but said nothing. He turned and headed toward the elevator, Scarlet in tow.

The wait for the Canadian authorities wasn't a lengthy one. Jason had moved the *Raven* to the narrow mouth of the inlet to ensure Bouchard and his men didn't escape into the open ocean. Sophia had managed to get Asako's wound cleaned up and had given her a mild sedative to help her sleep for a bit.

It turned out that Bouchard's men had raided the kitchen during their time aboard, so Jason fixed up a meager dinner out of what was left. He and Niles were clearing the table when three Canadian Coast Guard cutters entered the inlet, preceded by a military helicopter that buzzed overhead on its way toward the other boat.

"Jason, we're being hailed by the Canadian authorities," Oracle said.

Jason looked at everyone. "Okay, you all might as well get to tidying up." He motioned to the lounge, still in its very trashed state. He pointed to Niles. "You should probably join me since Asako is indisposed." He turned and headed for the stairs, "We can do this in my quarters. There's a working monitor."

WRAPPING UP

"The Canadians said Bouchard wasn't on the boat," Jason said, or rather repeated, for possibly the tenth time.

"I just don't understand how that's possible," Niles said, shaking his head. He poured another cup of coffee for himself. "We watched him take the tender over to his boat."

Jason shrugged. "I don't know what to tell you, Niles. They scoured the inlet and found nothing." Jason took a sip of his own coffee, then continued, "Best guess is he took the tender ashore, hid or sank it, and hoofed it into town then called for a ride." The South African man scowled but said nothing, instead sipping his coffee.

Two weeks had passed since the adventure on Graham Island. They'd returned Asako to Vancouver, where after a few days recuperating in her own bed, she'd submitted the very water-damaged papers she'd grabbed in the science labs of the old Japanese base to local museums for authentication. She has been fielding inquiries from museums and universities from around the world and doing a fair bit of debriefing with the Canadian *and* Japanese militaries ever since. The Japanese, for their part, were being open and honest as best they could. It turned out that anyone who knew about the base or the project had long since passed away so there wasn't much to share.

Niles had kept his own bounty of paperwork and trinkets from the base, and it was spread out on a worktable one floor down. Now that it was finally dry, it was time to catalog it all. He'd found a few museums that were interested in what he'd hastily grabbed. That, plus the payment from the University, meant the balance sheet for the job was in the black, which always made Jason happy, especially in light of the rather substantial repairs the *Raven* required. With the team's help, the virus in the University email server was found and erased. Unfortunately, there was no way to identify who'd placed it there, so the police let it drop after sharing what they had with every university that was interested, most were. Scarlet was able to confirm, almost certainly illegally, that the server that was receiving the intel from the universities was no longer on the internet.

"He heard us talking about the authorities. He knew his boat wasn't going anywhere and that if he stayed with it, he'd be arrested." Jason spread his hands. "Not our problem. We've still got to catalog all the offers on the table for your loot."

Niles took a sip of his coffee. "Something tells me we'll see Phillipe Bouchard again."

Before Jason could reply, Scarlet rolled in, a grin splitting her face. "Okay, so my delivery came while we were gone, right? It got redelivered—"

Jason held up a hand. "We've been here with you, we know. They dropped it off last night." He made a *go on* motion. "And?"

She made a face. "Right. Anyway, I was up all night setting it up. You gotta come see this." She didn't wait, turning and leaving the room.

Jason and Niles exchanged a glance and got up to follow their resident genius.

In the hall, they bumped into Sofia. "What's up?" she asked.

Scarlet spun her chair. "New toy show and tell."

The other woman shrugged and took Jason's coffee cup. "I got nothing else planned. *Vamos*." She extended a hand toward the elevator.

"I DON'T KNOW WHAT I'M LOOKING AT?" JASON SAID. THEY were in Scarlet's workshop in the outbuilding near the docks. In front of them was a massive framework of...something. There was a large circular platform in the center of the framework.

Scarlet rolled to her workbench and picked up a tablet. She tapped the device and the contraption that was taking up almost three-quarters of her workshop came to life. Several articulated arms unfolded and began working in the center of the device.

In only a few minutes, Jason saw what looked like a piece of aircraft fuselage taking shape. He pointed to it. "Is that..."

"A piece of an airplane?" Scarlet finished. She grinned. "Yeah." She waved the table toward the large device whirring away. "Large-scale industrial 3D printer." She pointed to several large tanks and racks attached to the back of the machine. "Raw materials. Metal sheet and ore."

Niles whistled. "While this is impressive, dear, why are you making an airplane?"

Sofia elbowed the portly South African. "Who cares? We're going to have an airplane." She looked at the piece of fuselage being assembled. "Someday."

The End.

I hope you enjoyed this first adventure of Jason and the Expedition, Inc. Team. I'm excited to see where in the world they find their next adventure! I hope you'll come along!

Keep an eye out for book two, "Dangerous Baggage" Late 2022.

Reviews are the lifeblood of indie authors. If you could take a minute to leave a review, it'd mean the world to me. Don't know what to say? "I liked it." Is a perfectly fine review to leave.

Did I mention how much social proof is worth to indie authors? :)

OFFER

As they say, there's no harm in asking, so here we go.

If you can help connect me with someone who can get Expedition Inc. on a screen (Big or Little) I'll cut you in for 10% (Up to $10,000) of whatever advance is paid.

Send me an email and we can discuss.
rights@johnwilker.com

Want to stay up to date on the adventures of the Expedition Inc team?
Sign up for my newsletter
Or visit me online at
johnwilker.com

I've loved writing since I was a kid. I entered writing contests in 2nd and 3rd grade. I read books and wrote book reports for my parents (It helped that I got a new G.I. Joe for each book report). From that point on I've told stories wherever I could.

Growing up on Indiana Jones, he was bound to rub off on me. Add to that a little known (sadly) Canadian TV show called, "Adventure, Inc." really stoked the creative fires as a kid.

I hope to keep telling the story of Jason and his friends for as long as people enjoy reading them.

Tell your friends, tell your family, tell the person next to you on the plane that just looked at you funny for laughing out loud. You see where I'm going with this. :)

OTHER BOOKS BY J. BECKETT (JOHN WILKER)

I write Action/Adventure Thrillers as J. Beckett. I write science fiction under John Wilker.

The Space Rogues Series. Wil Calder and a bunch of alien misfits somehow keep finding themselves in the thick of it. No one ever checks qualifications when it comes to saving the galaxy!

The Grand Human Empire Series. Jax, Naomi and the droids are just trying to get by. New droid parts ain't cheap after all.